Boomerang!

THE ENVIRO KIDS

NEVILLE BAGNALL

Grosvenor House
Publishing Limited

The right of Neville Bagnall to be identified as the author of this
work has been asserted in accordance with Section 78
of the Copyright, Designs and Patents Act 1988

The book cover is copyright to Neville Bagnall

This book is published by
Grosvenor House Publishing Ltd
Link House
140 The Broadway, Tolworth, Surrey, KT6 7HT.
www.grosvenorhousepublishing.co.uk

This book is a work of fiction. Any resemblance to
people or events, past or present, is purely coincidental.

A CIP record for this book
is available from the British Library

ISBN 978-1-80381-945-7
eBook ISBN 978-1-80381-946-4

Author Biography

Neville Bagnall lives in Llanelli, south Wales. He studied BSc (Hons) in health, safety and environmental management and MSc in sustainable business risk management. His work includes teaching about protecting the environment which gave him the idea to put into his writing. He highlights the real environmental challenges everyone faces today in the hope of a cleaner climate for the children in their future tomorrows and beyond.

In 'Boomerang!', Neville exposes the real dangers of not protecting the environment from the invisible *ninja* pollutants. Boomerang! is the second book in the Enviro Kids series adventures exploring environmental impacts all around our planet Earth.

Dedications

To my children who fill the days with smiles, compassion, love, patience and demands... and even more demands! I wonder if there are snippets of them in the characters in this book.

And to those whose actions to protect the environment are resourceful, meaningful, genuine, and selfless. The children of today will have pride in these people...

...but not to those who have no shame like governments who give empty promises and the big corporations who choose profit and greed by polluting our planet. Their children will not be so proud.

Acknowledgments

I would like to thank Grosvenor House Publishers for their faith in the concept of *Boomerang!* and its environmental message. Also, thanks to the editorial department for giving the book's content the opportunity to be made available for publication. Further thanks to everyone in the production team who have been so supportive throughout the process and for producing the creative and illuminating cover design.

CHAPTER 1

Land Of Dreams

Streaky streams of beaming light puncture through the treetop canopy of the high-reaching lanky trees. The sparkling light shines down brightly into Katty's eyes like dazzling spotlights through the canopy covering of the treetops. She gawps in awe at the trees as they stretch and stretch really high up into the sky. The tree's branches reach out to the branches of other trees, and they intertwine as they hold onto each other, huddling together underneath the lush dark green treetop covering. Katty had entered a different world. It felt free but with an air of mystery too. It felt like the forest was filled with magical spirits from a different time. It was like something out of *Jurassic Park*. She gulps and hopes there are no nasty roaming dinosaurs lurking in the rainforest. Her mind twizzles. *Wow!*

'This is awesome,' Katty coos. Her head spins in bliss. She can't believe she is actually stood in the middle of the Amazon rainforest. *Phew!* She puffs out her cheeks. *Wowzer!* She gawps, open mouthed at the magnificent trees stretching high up into the sky.

'Shut your mouth, Katty,' bleats a smirking Jake. 'You might catch flies in that big gob!' Katty snaps her mouth shut tight. She scowls at her annoying little brother. She wished his mouth were shut… permanently. He always had too much to say. He should respect his older sister. But he didn't. He was a 'mummy's boy' and that it made it even worse for her.

'Look down at your feet, Jake,' growls Katty. Jake squints a frown and looks down to the ground.

'Why?' he asks.

'Can't you see your friends?' smirks Katty.

'Huh? Friends?' Jake frowns again.

'Why don't you get into the dirt,' she teases, 'like the little worm you are.'

'Oh! Just because Miss Violet couldn't come with us, you don't have to get all niggly and nasty,' scowls Jake. 'Anyways, it is the big worms crawling up your legs you should be scared about. They call them snakes.'

Katty shudders and sticks out her tongue at her smug little know-it-all brother. Katty was not happy that Miss Violet, her science schoolteacher, was not with them and Katty couldn't understand what was more important for Miss than going to the Amazon rainforest.

Last night, they had touched down on the airport's floodlit, smooth, glistening, black tarmac runway. They had finally arrived. They had floated through the sky like the amazing, migrating Whooper swans they had passed on the way up. The only difference was they were on an aeroplane, and, in Katty's case, she was going in search for answers to a very big problem. She was really excited about this new *real* adventure. She recalled that Miss Violet had reminded her, in the science laboratory at Brumfield Primary school, the day before Katty's plane took off that not everything would be pleasant, even though it was an adventure. It was an exploration too. It was an adventure with purpose, decided Katty. It was a team adventure together as the 'Enviro Kids'. That meant her and her annoying, gobby, babbling, know-it-all younger brother, Jake. Mum and Dad had to tag along too!

Katty realised, thanks to Miss, that it would be important to witness the amazing natural beauty of the Amazon rainforest for what it is, and for what was wrong too. She knew that she would have to witness the deforestation damage for what it is too. It was her task to explore and find out the *real* story of the Amazon rainforest. Katty had noticed how Miss Violet gasped and gulped at the thought of what lay ahead for Katty and Jake.

Katty hummed as she pondered with frowning uncertainty. She didn't know if Miss's gulp meant whether it was for better or for worse. Katty now gulped. *Crikey!* she fretted. Either way, she was here now, and she would soon find out for herself.

The flight took them almost half a day and they had travelled a whopping six thousand miles. With droopy tired eyes, they were shuttled into a double decker open air truck. Katty thought it was a bit like a safari jeep-bus type thing – but without the roaming lions, giraffes, and elephants anywhere nearby. The truck had trundled bumpily along the winding dirt track through to the edges of the mighty, ginormous Amazon rainforest. Katty found it impossible to get too excited because her body was knackered, zapped of energy and her mind was only just about ticking over. Mum called it 'jet lag.' Jake called it zombified! Soon Katty would be actually living in the Amazon rainforest. It was unreal and she somehow managed to saunter out of the double decker truck still standing upright even though she was bruised, befuddled and exhausted. She was a walking zombie homing in on a soft mattress that was calling her name. The low torch-like sun slunk droopily into the fuzzy horizon and a blanket of murky, dusky darkness folded down through the tops of the trees' forest canopy. Katty gawped at the super-duper lanky trees that stretch upwards into the dark, nighttime duvet settling down from the clouds.

The camp was a small open space which greeted them as they wearily carried their rucksacks and bags. There were pairs of log cabins perched on little stumpy legs that wore straw hats for roofs with steps leading up to a seated porchway. It looked inviting in her weariness. The cabins formed a semi-circle, and the river was shimmering about 20 metres ahead of them, just a short stretch away. It felt deserted in a peaceful, calm and welcoming way. Katty could feel her eyes drooping heavily and her shoulders sagged. She was seriously tired. Katty, Jake, Mum and Dad scoffed down a bowl of pork and vegetable stew with dumplings. Katty ate in silence like everyone else. She had a quick wash, cleaned her teeth and it was straight to bed, tucked in by Mum and Dad and shielded by mosquito netting hanging all around the bed frame. Mosquito nets were draped over each bed and even the windows and doors were screened with mesh.

A whirring buzz hums, whirs, purrs and zips around inside Katty's head. *Do mosquitoes really buzz? That can't be right*, she questions. Mosquitoes are silent bloodsuckers who want to devour her blood in slurps and gulps. *Urgh! Just like vampires.*

'Oh, yuk!' she gags, sticking her tongue out.

Katty hardly notices anything inside or around the cabin. She slept like a log... in a log cabin. It was like being in a strange but peaceful and sleeping zoo... at least until tomorrow.

Katty and Jake slept in their separate bedrooms in the wood hut eco lodge, and Mum and Dad shared another. Shiny, shaded wood decorated the floors, walls and ceilings, giving the cabin rooms a pleasant wooden, rose-like scent. It had a smoky yet sweet fragrance, sniffed Katty. The campsite of five lodges were placed in a small clearing near the riverbank with a short pier protruding out into the water. The silhouette of a riverboat was moored up alongside the pier.

* * * * * *

Breakfast had been the same as many breakfast tables across Brazil: jam and soft crunchy toast as part of their first meal of the day. Each toasted bread slice was the size of a brick, but it was soft. A thick layer of sweet grape jam was spread across the toast. *Yummy! Scrummy!* It was so chewy and very filling, declared Katty by rubbing her satisfied tummy.

Sergio, their tour guide, arrived just as they finished breakfast. Katty and Jake had been tucking into their banana jam on a slab of toasted bread and swilling it down with an olive green, slimy looking drink. It looked disgusting at first, but it tasted a bit like vanilla. It was something like avocado blended with milk and sugar. *Tasty*, Jake had proclaimed as he gulped down another glassful into his gullet. Sergio strode closer and Katty thought he looked about twenty-something, too young to be a guide, not really knowing what to expect. His short dark hair kinked in curls, and he had a wide, pearly white smile.

Sergio's eyes lock on to Katty's as he folds his arms across his chest, cocks his head to one side and frowns. Katty instantly thought he was telepathic. *Oh no*, she fretted, *he is just like Mum*, reading her mind and knowing what she is thinking and what she is going to do. *Seriously, this can't be good.* Her cheeks blush. He frowns and smirks.

'Are you wearing a wig?' asks Sergio. Katty coughs in shock. *What?* her mind screams. Jake's eyebrows spring up, his eyes wide open.

'Sorry?' Katty splutters. 'Excuse me. A wig? Do you think this is a wig?' Her hand grasps and tugs down at her fringe.

'Oh, you know, you are an environmental campaigner like Greta Thunberg, and she has pigtails hanging down,' stutters Sergio. Jake is loving this awkward chat with a crooked, sly smile as he looks at Katty.

'Yeah, piggy tails is about right. Oink! Oink!' quips Jake. Katty's eyes narrow as she scowls.

'Shut up, Jake. It's plaited hair, not piggity tails. You prat,' she snaps, 'and you don't have to have plaited hair if you want to campaign for the environment either, Sergio!'

'Ah, okay. Of course not. Sorry Katty,' Sergio says with an apologetic nod.

Jake looks from Sergio to Katty, and he nods too.

'Yeah. Sergio's sorry, but I'm not, Miss Piggy-tails! Oink! Oink,' snorts Jake.

After hours of carefully trekking through the hot, sweaty forest, Katty realises that her hearing has become zoned into the surroundings. With her cat-like, sonar ears she picks up every crackle, squeak, whistle, bark and moan. The whinging was Jake. He was sniffling and groaning about the non-stop walking and that there was no big, juicy hamburger in sight... or smell. Even the long pauses of eerie silence grab Katty's attention. She could see Jake just ahead of her, stomping clumsily without a care in the world, probably daydreaming in a world of his own. Only Mario racing his kart in the rainforest would catch Jake's attention... or a big, fat juicy hamburger! Beads of sweat trickle down Katty's face like a spring waterfall from her drenched, grey headband. She had to take it off and wring out the damp, humid air that soaked it. If only she had a hairdryer to sort it out. All their clothes had to be light in colour because the mosquitoes are attracted to dark clothes. And she was definitely not having that!

She wore khaki cream trousers with zips and pockets on the front, side and back - even more room to pack snack bars. She wore a beige, long-sleeved polo shirt, buttoned up to a light grey neck snood. She blinks and blows out with puffed cheeks. Katty wonders what the chirping parrots, barking monkeys and hissing snakes think about these intruders. Do they think that she, Jake, Mum, Dad and Sergio are more loggers coming to chop down their habitat? Or do they think they are farmers coming to burn down their worldly existence to flatten the land to farm crop and to feed cattle? Maybe the chirps, barks and hisses are calls of distress. *Umm*, she ponders, covering her mouth with her hand. Perhaps they were shouting naughty, swear words like Mum does when someone has stolen one of her favourite chocolate brownies. She was always putting them in one of her secret hiding places like in the bottom of the bran flakes cereal box or even left in the oven.

The threat of loggers, ranchers and farmers freak out the macaws, monkeys and snakes. *Doomed!* fret the squawking birds. Doomed to more burning, chopping and destroying of their home. Doomed to more deforestation.

'*No more deforestation*,' rings out from high above in the trees as a choir of squealing toucans, squawking macaws and hooting, barking owls trill out in chorus.

The loggers, ranchers and farmers chop and burn down the rainforest. That, Katty fretted, was gnawing away at the home of the monkeys, toucans and macaws, and stripping them of their home and their existence.

Jake wondered if he could teach the macaws to repeat some words for him. He tuts to himself in amusement. *Where's the brownies, Mum? – Squawk. Where's the brownies, Mum? – Squawk*, the macaws screech. Jake sniggers at the thought. He knows Mum would not be impressed. It was like when Jake repeatedly pestered Mum by asking her where she is going. Mum would reply she was going '*off her head*' with him pestering her. He found that funny too.

Katty lay in bed with her mosquito net securely in place. Her brain was running on empty. The day was filled with the taste of foods, the smells and noises of the trees and animals, the landscape and the glorious colours of an awesome forest. She needed sleep. Her aching eyelids flutter and droop shut. The darkness prompts the melatonin in her brain to gently sweep her conscious mind into a deep, slumbering doze. The jet lag consumed her body into a curled up slump and heavy snooze. Tomorrow, she would be more awake with her eyes wide open to savour more of one of the natural wonders of the world.

CHAPTER 2

Whoosh, Bang, Wallop!

Katty's eyes creak dozily open. She'd survived the night without being bitten by the vampire mosquitoes. She had thought about wearing a garlic necklace to ward off the vampires, but she was glad that the mosquito net had done its job. She was bite-free, and she would make sure she stays that way too. The mosquito repellent was sprayed on her hands, and she carefully rubs the moist repellent onto her face. She also sprays the repellent onto her clothing, in and around her sleeve cuffs, socks and around the tops of her trekking boots. Just like Sergio the guide had told her. She was determined to stay bite-free during another day of hot, sticky walking and another day of exploring the jungle. Their daily jaunts routine meant that first thing, they put on their thick woolly socks and get into their chunky all-terrain, roughie-toughie hiking boots. Katty and Jake rummaged through their compact rucksacks, checking everything was in place.

Mosquito spray – *check*, mosquito cream – *check*, sunblock – *check*, chocolate biscuits – *check*. Mum had managed to make some soggy brownies. *No one would be stealing any of these soggy brownies*, reckons Katty. Still, it was food. They were hardly going on a picnic.

Sergio taps his hand on top of Katty and Jake's shoulders and reminds them to tuck their trouser bottoms into their socks.

'Roll your socks right up over the bottom of your trousers,' Sergio would bark out, 'so there is less chance of a snake bite or something crawling up your leg.'

Katty shudders and her eyes bulge right out into a wide-eyed, crazy stare. She pulls the tops of her socks over her trousers. Jake pulls a *yuk* face. Sergio, Mum and Dad kept on warning them about mosquito bites. The words of warning literally buzz and hum into their ears. It started off with instructions from the lady travel agent to wear neutral-coloured clothing. It would have to be beige or light grey – mosquitoes are attracted to dark colours so it would be useless for Katty to wear her green, velvety beret and any matching superhero, bright green leotard and cape outfit. This was a symbol of her environment crusade. She'd look like 'Kermit the Frog', as Jake had teased her about it during their last school campaign. That was Katty and Jake's first campaign. That was to stop parents from not switching off their car engines because when they lazily idle their car engines when outside of school, the car engines spew out exhaust fumes filled with disgusting pollutants.

What they had to wear now were boring, long-sleeved, breathable garments so they were covered up from the mozzies. *Huh!* Those yukky, pesky mosquitoes and any other menacing, flying insects. *Do this, do that; don't do this, don't do that.* Finger wagging instructions came from all directions – Mum, Dad, Sergio. Katty even imagined a howler monkey wagging its finger at her too and telling her to put on insect repellent.

Katty sprays the insect repellent wildly. It was like being in a hair salon and getting smothered in a cloud of spray. Katty and Jake panic and fret so much about the mosquitos that if they spot any exposed skin, they make sure they slap more cream on, spurting it on and on, again and again. They sprayed again on their outer clothing to deter the pesky mozzies. Wrinkling her nose, it was hardly what Katty would call nice smelling deodorant, she cringed. She puffed out her cheeks. It was *her* against the irritating, blood slurping munchers buzzing in and around her, just waiting to dive in and suck on her blood. Oh, gross. *Urgh!* she gagged. She shivered and quaked at the thought of the gleeful, blood-slurping mozzies having a feast at her expense. She didn't want to catch malaria. She shuddered. It seemed a never-ending battle between the human and the mosquitoes.

Whoosh, bang, wallop, slap, swish… splat, splat.

Katty and Jake would swiftly shut and slam every door and window screen in the cabin to stop any chance of the annoying mozzies getting into their safe shelter. Luckily, she sighed in relief, the cabins were air-conditioned as Sergio had said that mosquitoes don't like cold or flowing air. *Huh!* Katty and Jake were taking no chances and insisted on draping the mosquito nets over their beds to keep the little blood sucking mites at bay. Sergio had laughed, mosquitoes don't hum but they do buzz and bite. *Better safe than sorry*, Mum had said. Dad just smirked and shrugged his shoulders. Dad was so brave. If he went to the doctors for whatever illness, he would come back and say that the doctor had remarked at how brave he was. *Brave!? As if Dad could be brave*, Mum had quipped. She knew that every time he went to donate blood, he fainted! He was such an attention seeker, she guffawed.

Jake asks Sergio whether they should wear camouflage make-up for their jungle tour. Sergio thinks he has misunderstood Jake but is not sure and thinks it might be an English expression. Katty grins.

'You don't wear make-up for school or when you go out playing Jake. And you're defo not using mine,' she says.

'Uh! What?' groans Jake. 'Are you bonkers? I didn't mean make-up like that. I meant camouflage so we can't be spotted by the enemy.'

'You have to wear light coloured clothes. Else the mosquitoes fly around and do dive-bomb attacks and cover you like a swarm of bees doing their blood-sucking vampire impressions,' points out Katty annoyingly, poking her tongue out for good measure.

The rainforest reminded Katty of stepping into a different world like Narnia, she thought. Within a couple of minutes of leaving the camp, they were trudging into the depths of the rainforest again. A curtain wall of trees reached up to the skies. The spindly, spider-leg like roots of the trees stuck out above the ground. Katty climbs over and stands in between them. They spread out at the bottom of the tree like giant spider's legs, sprawling all around.

It reminded Jake of the forest in *The Lord of the Rings*. *Oh, wow!* his mind spun. He could actually be surrounded by real walking, talking trees. He sniggered under his breath. *Could these trees really talk?* He doubted it. The trees went up and up and up, way high up into the clear blue sky. It made Jake's neck ache to look up trying to see the tops of the trees as they touched the sky.

Katty's heart skips a beat. *Huh!* she gasps. She was sure her brain heard murmurings and whispers from not so high up in the canopy. A peculiar thought prickled her mind and the cogwheels in her head turned and spun. After a few more clunks, clicks, and a little whirring she was sure someone or something was talking. It brought back something Sergio had said about the trees being able to walk. The palm trees do a really slow walk to get out of the shade and into the sun. Crawling tree roots is what Sergio said made the trees walk. Walking trees! Shock! Sergio even suggested that other trees, known as Mystrees, were real walking, talking trees and that they possessed wizardry abilities. Could Katty imagine trees doing a slow dance? Crikey! How long would that take? The Mystrees were not impressed with Katty's sarcastic slow dance thoughts. Wizards could read minds telepathically, much like Katty's Mum! *If it was the trees talking, then what were they talking about?* Katty thought with suspicion. The trees gave her the jitters.

'Huh!' huff the trees.

'Yes, wee's can walks, you stupidsy tourists,' protested laid-back Lofty from his elevated and very tall Mystree position. He was way up high in the forest's canopy.

'Chill out, Lofty,' quips the whinging Spike – a not so tall Mystree who likes nothing better than to moan about everything. Spike spat out, 'you're not exactly speedy Gonzalez!'

'I moves as quicks as I can and I don't dooz slow dances,' Lofty splutters a chuckle.

'Brrrr. Those tourists give me the jibblie-jibblies,' huffs Spike. 'I don't trust them.'

Sergio leans his head down to both Katty and Jake, his eyes peering from side to side as he quietly whispers to them a secret of the rainforest.

'Be very careful what you say about the rainforest,' whispers Sergio. He holds his index finger up to his lips and has a quick glance over his shoulder. Katty and Jake look at each other. 'Remember,' utters Sergio. 'Some of the trees walk amongst the jungle and they have ears and talk to each other.' Sergio pauses, his eyes flinch. 'And they can cast magical spells too.' Jake's jaw drops open like a medieval drawbridge. Katty frowns. Her eyes twitch and squint. She is filled with confusion and a bit of doubt. *Walking, talking trees. Really? That's doesn't seem right*, her mind queried. Sergio's whispers drew an eerie silence. Spooky. Katty noticed that there were no birds twirping, no rustling branches… there was nothing to be exact.

'There's a real myth of wizardry trees in the rainforest. They are known as *Mystrees*,' murmurs Sergio. He explains how the walking, talking trees move through the forest and dense foliage tiptoeing on their creaking, crackling roots. The twanging noise of branches collide as the Mystrees shuffle between the trees. Katty's eyes widened as Sergio told of how the Mystrees seek out and cast spells on undesirables like loggers, rascal farmers, ranchers and even misbehaving tourists. He'd never seen a Mystree, but he knew they were nearby because of the murmuring, swirling breezes whistling through the rainforest followed by a ghostly silence.

'What kind of spells do they put on tourists, Sergio?' gulps Jake. 'Because I've been really good. I haven't misbehaved at all. I promise,' he stammered a quaking whisper whilst peering up towards the canopy for any sign of movement or murmuring of trees who might be hatching a plan to cast a spell on him. Katty pursed her lips. *The lying little worm*, she vexes. She bet Mum would like to cast a spell on him if she could. She could already read their minds with her telepathic powers. 'I know what you're thinking', she would snap, and she was always right. It proper spooked Katty and Jake out with their eyes popping out of their pale, startled faces.

As Katty looked up, arching her neck back, she squinted high up into the far-reaching Kapok trees enwrapped in a light blanket of mist. She imagines the Mystrees chattering away amongst themselves. They could be talking about them as mischievous tourists, or they could be admiring the views across the tops of the trees' canopy. Either way, she hoped they would not cast any spells on her.

'Hey, Lofty, the clammy mist is making me itch and sweat,' whines Spike.

'It'll rain soon 'cos that's what we dooz. Wee's the ones whatsis creates the rain. 'Tis a fact; 'tis what we dooz. You knows that. Don't be stupidsy. Just be patient,' garbles Lofty as his wrinkly, bark skin quivers in the dense mist. He twitches and itches a little too. He reaches out one of his branches and scratches the cleft of his trunk where a harpy eagle had been nesting, digging and scratching its talons into *his* bark.

Katty can imagine the Mystrees asking for help and getting all emotional, stressed and suffering in pain – burns, scorching, singed leaves and charred branches. It must be awful even for the Mystrees to witness other trees suffering and disappearing as the loggers chop them down. The remaining stubby stumps jutting out of the ground could be tree headstones in a cemetery. Headstone stumps reflect the loving memory of what was once a forestry thicket of thriving, photosynthetic carbon-absorbing trees.

A strained, tense grin creases Katty's face. She peers up again into the wispy, wavery blanket of mist that was now obscuring the whispering, lanky trees. Sergio saw them as mystical trees without shadows – you never knew they were there. *All that hot, sticky mist must be like being in a sauna*, mused Katty. The Mystrees had plenty to complain about. Mum always seemed to complain about something and someone. And it was always something to do with Dad! And the Mystrees did have a lot to whinge about at times, especially if there was the threat of fire and being chopped down by loggers wanting more wood to sell. A breezy waft of watery air whizzed past Katty's head. *What was all that about?* she frowned in deep thought.

'A-a-a-tish-oooo,' sneezed lazy Lofty as a dribble of snot trickled from his nose down into the crevices of his bark skin.

'Bless you! Lofty,' whispers prickly Spike in a sarcastic tone, much to Lofty's annoyance. Lofty was as patient as he was easy-going, but he did find Spike's constant mocking, nastiness and whinging a bit irritating at times. 'Have you caught the flu, Lofty?' sneers Spike with a sly grin. 'You rickety rotting, crumbling, wrinkly old excuse for a Kapok tree.'

'No,' Lofty huffed and sniffled. His squinting eyes peer down to Spike. 'I haven't gots the flu. You is just an irritating sap-leaking, bark-infested, stinking planks of woods,' splutters Lofty, 'and I'm not old either. I'm only two hundred years old. I've gots another one hundred years of growth yet.' Lofty sniffles, snuffles and swipes a bark-sleeved branch across his nose.

'Huh!' huffs Spike. 'So why are you dribbling snot all over the place then?'

'I dunno,' wheezes Lofty with a heavy grunting sigh. 'I thinks I'm allergics to the mist. Or else… I'm allergics to you!'

Spike scowls in protest, huffs and rolls his knotted eyes.

The mist reminded Katty of when Gramps had pointed to the pollutant-filled thick quilted blanket of city smog outside his house. The smog menacingly lingered and choked the air. She now knows that the polluted mist could be in any town or city in the world. But this mist was not because of exhaust fumes from the heavy traffic. This mist was different.

Katty knew the Mystrees were close by and talking but she couldn't make sense of any the whispering chitter-chatter way up above her head. The whispers could have been Portuguese, Spanish, English or any language – she had no clue. The whispery mumblings still didn't make sense. She would have asked Sergio, but he was in discussion with Jake about playing a Mario Kart game sometime. What Sergio didn't know was that Jake would be cheating like he always does. Katty rolled her eyes and shook her head. *Boys will be boys!*

On the forest floor, through a thicket of trees, Katty can see an agouti. She can only describe it as a large guinea pig with long legs. The agouti was foraging amongst the leaves and started to nibble on an avocado that had dropped as a gift from the tree food store above. *It was easier than shopping with a trolley and scanning the barcode at the till*, muses Katty. *A bit like cooked food being delivered to the house – no foraging, no queuing, no cooking – no inconvenience. The agouti has the food at its feet!*

A waft of dirty air fills the forest. Katty's eyes smart and tingle. She squints hard. Her nostrils twang at a yukky, smoky smell. The misty air became a thick, dense cloud. In less than a minute, the dirty cloud shut out the view of tree-tops and consumed the oxygen all around her. She splutters and chokes. She covers her mouth and nose with her snood. The air was now a mass fervour of filthy pollutants. Pollutants of burning charred wood, soot and smoke. The skies above were obscured from view by a murky stinking darkness. A waft of smoke weaves in between the trees and slithers like a ghostly, black demonic snake, hissing its way through the rainforest's dense, ginormous thicket of trees. The stench of acrid smoke clung to the back of Katty's throat as she gagged and rubbed at her stinging eyes. The rainforest was on fire… again. The plumes of smoke are belched out, carrying blankets of cloud-speckled black soot. The smoke drapes over like a magician's cloak, laying down a black carpet and masking the bright blue sky's beaming sun rays. Katty gags and splutters as she desperately tries to resist the unpleasant smoke from choking her throat and burning her lungs. The coughs and splutters echo around as they all huddled up together. Forest lungs contracting – alveoli dying, less oxygen flowing, hearts beating faster, chests heaving, frantically wheezing and gasping in clumps of dirty air. It was like when she was choking in the back of Mum's car from the traffic exhaust fumes when they were in the city. It was happening all over again but this time six thousand miles away in the middle of a continental-sized rainforest. Déjà vu! Boomerang! And not in a good way.

'Crouch down,' bellows Sergio. 'Get down low. Turn your face away and cover your mouth and nose.' The plumes of smoke dance, swirl, weave and wrap around every branch, twig and human as is tumbles and rolls along the forest floor. They were suffocating in the underlay to a smoke drenched stinking carpet. Katty wonders if all the animals have scarpered up the trees to get fresh air. It was as though a weight of guilt was pressing her down; she knew the pollutants were literally all around her, including in the form of black stinking soot. She flung her arms up in despair with clenched fists and gritted teeth.

'Why doesn't this matter to the rest of the world?' mumbles Jake. His eyebrows scrunch towards his squinted eyes. If the Amazon rainforest is supposed to be the lungs of the Earth, so Sergio the guide had said only yesterday during breakfast, then the lungs of the Earth are choking *their* throats today. That's a lot of bad charred ash smouldering and spewing out bad breath, heaving out zillions of bad pollutants.

The lungs of the Earth, Jake remembers. Photosynthesis in the Amazon rainforest is on a mega, super-duper, ginormous scale. But the vast burning and chopping of trees means less photosynthesis and the lungs of the Earth are wheezing, gasping for carbon dioxide to turn into oxygen. To burn the trees releases pollution into the air and takes away what absorbs the carbon dioxide. Miss Violet had explained that when the wood burns, it releases smoke and gases in the form of carbon dioxide.

'Yukky carbon dioxide,' coughed Jake. He recognised the rancid, splattering sooty ash. It's a vicious cycle;

a double whammy. It's a catastrophic head-banging nightmare that badly affects the whole world, and Jake's head was pounding like mad. It was proper Boomerang! *If you burn down trees then it's gonna whirl back like a boomerang does and pollute the air.* It was proper mad, he fumed.

Katty could see that Jake's stare was blank and vacant. He'd gone into one again. His brain was overwhelmed with disbelief. She knew he would re-boot his brain in a minute and reset to the same old Jake. *Yep*, she sighed. The same old annoying little worm, rat, know-it-all, no respect for his older sister Jake. She looked at Mum accusingly because no matter what argument took place between Katty and Jake, Mum would say she should know better, and of course, Jake was always innocent. Pity. *Yeah right*. Katty bit her lower lip like what Taylor Swift would do to stop her frustration from showing. *You need to calm down*, Katty urges herself, *you're being too loud...* Jake. Katty managed a little lopsided smirk to herself and sighed again. This time it was a half-happy sigh toward Jake.

Everything they touched was layered in black soot. It was same when Gramps told them to touch the garden wall in the city filled with smoke-spluttering traffic. There was the same black soot smeared on all the buildings. Pollutants everywhere. Even far away in another part of the world in South America. Brazil to be precise. The Amazon rainforest. Full of awesome natural beauty and now the same old mucky 'black carbon' soot.

Katty and Jake recognised the dirty black soot. They'd seen these pollutants before. Car exhaust fumes spilling out stinking pollutants. The soot festering all around them and the pollutants drifting up into the air, high up into the atmosphere causing havoc with the ozone layer. They would definitely be going on a space exploration adventure to check out what damage the pollutants were doing to the ozone layer. But for now, they were seeing first-hand what the problems were with the Amazon rainforest. And it wasn't good, Katty fretted.

'Déjà vu,' murmurs Jake. He'd heard Miss Violet use this expression on the back of 'oh no, not again'. He didn't think she said it about him not doing his homework on time, but it might have been. *Oh yes, it makes sense now.* He thinks it was something like experiencing something now which had also happened before, and now it was happening all over again. It was something like that, he decided. The soot was here again. The pollutants were here again, and it would repeat itself with the pollutants coming back again and again. It was just like Sergio had said. Just like Sergio's watery eyes of hopelessness and despair came back, time and time again. Just like world leaders and politicians promising change but lying, time and time again. Mum says that about her chocolate brownies disappearing, time and time again, no matter where she hides them. And there are the repeated lies, time and time again. And that if Dad lies and there are brownies missing, then there will be big trouble; Mum had sternly warned everyone… especially Dad. Jake and Katty smirked. Dad's left eyebrow rose, he blushed a little, but Mum didn't notice.

Katty had overheard Sergio blaming their own president for encouraging the stealing of wood and land from the Amazon rainforest by loggers, ranchers, farmers and miners. Could Katty smell another whiff of smoke in the air? She wasn't sure, the tangy musky smell lingered in the air and filled her nostrils. The taste of pollution was everywhere.

The pollutants hang in the air. The cacophony of yelps, screams and whinging drift up into the atmosphere and more pollutants float down towards the ground, splattering and smudging every surface with their dirty, stinking, slimy black soot. Toxie the pollutant was miffed. It would be a battle to find a clear surface to land on. The pollutants jostled in mid-air for a clear descent, but it was impossible. Rumbling yelps and grunts of irritation and anger rang in Toxie's ears as the pollutants bump into each other, scrambling without hope. There were just too many of them. At this rate, they would be landing on top of each other making thick dense layers of soot all around and creating a thick piled carpet of black grimy dust.

Toxie whooshes up from the flames like a phoenix dragon, or so he would like to think. The inferno heat was spitting crackling embers from the trees and scattering them everywhere. He quickly propels clear of the bright red and orange flames licking at the trees below. There is no light, just a swirling darkness, as his body tumbles in the current of the thick billowing smoke. All he can see are thousands and thousands of pairs of pollutant, beady eyes blinking in distress and confusion. The beady eyes throng amongst the blanket of swirling plumes of smoke. Toxie could see that the other pollutants' blinking eyes flicker, quicker and quicker. The smoke engulfs their vision, stinging and reddening their eyes. He couldn't blink clearly any longer.

Toxie feels like he is swimming against the tide through the swirling smoke currents and he is being swept up and he drops back down into the dense billowing smoke clouds. He can't see a thing, he fumes. Well, apart from the blur of thousands of pairs of the now blinking bloodshot eyes. He is flying blind. He is startled as there is a grab onto his right hand. The grip tightens and he instinctively reaches out with his left hand and clamps onto another pollutant's hand. Tamin, another pollutant, gasps and shudders in relief. They are facing each other – eyeballs to eyeballs through the blustering swirling blackness. They are spinning in tandem, holding on tight for the dear dirty contaminated lives. The rollercoaster ride stops without warning like they've entered some sort of vortex vacuum. Their stomachs flip-flop, somersault and jump up into their throats as they drop like stones and keep dropping through the black, smouldering abyss.

'Oh no!,' cries Toxie, panic etched across his ashen face. 'If only I had a parachute.'

'What, really? Just the one parachute, do you mean?' snapped Tamin.

He fretted at the inevitable kerflop and kerplunk onto the tree stump. It was a thud, splosh and a gooey dunking. The landing was soft and splodgy. He had landed on top of a tree stump that was swimming in weeping sap. And so, of course, had Tamin. She was still fretting at Toxie's selfish one parachute jibe. The sap was gurgling and boiling under the intense fire and heat.

'Yuk and double yuk,' splutters Tamin, followed by a throaty gargle and wrenching cough.

Chapter 3

Daydreams

There was something vaguely familiar in the air and settling all around her, Katty sensed. She peers and squints at the black speckled air. After the fire and billowing smoke, the pollutants are showering down, crashing on the trees, the ground, floating in the river and settling on top of Katty, Jake and the others. The pollutants crash and splatter into the trees like Katty had remembered the pollutants splatting into the buildings in the city. Gramps had pointed out to Katty and Jake about the black soot on the brickwork of the houses and how the soot had smeared onto their fingers when they rubbed them against the garden wall. The same smudge of black sooty pollutants smeared again, only now it was embedded into the bark of the trees and covering their exposed leg-like roots. It was all too familiar to Katty and Jake, whether it was outside their school in the city centre with Gramps and Grandma or here in Brazil's Amazon rainforest. *How weird was that?* she vexed sadly. She slowly pirouetted on her toes like an awkward ballerina dancer as she continued to look up, down and around at the showering speckly descent of soot.

It felt gloomy.

Sergio waved his arms and escorted the group away from the choking smoke and smearing soot into clearer air. Sergio leads them trudging further and further away to safety. All they could do is steer clear from the smouldering smoke and soot. Sergio scribbled a note of where the smouldering location was to pass on to the police to come and check out for criminal activities.

Katty imagines a different world without pollution where people care more for the forests, the trees and the animals who live there. It suddenly struck her that humans should treat the animals as friends – then they would have more of a chance to survive and not to burn down their homes. She had an urge to hug a tree and she didn't care who saw her do it either.

She stepped forward and gently leaned against a tree. She sighed and closed her eyes. She didn't care if the tree was *prickly* Spike or *laid-back* Lofty. Her body just had to lean against them. She wanted them to know she was there for them. Spike would have a whinge and pretend not to care and Lofty would give a crusty bark-crackling grin.

'Maybe the touristsy girl is not so bads after all,' splutters Lofty pertly.

'There's no such thing as a *good* tourist. They don't belong here,' grunts Spike, spitting out a splintered piece of bark in disgust.

Katty startled and gave Sergio a frozen stare. She thought she heard a gravelly, hoarse growl from somewhere in the undergrowth. And she thought it was close by too. Sergio held out his outstretched hand, nodded to her and beckoned her to come next to him. She sprung out a few quick-step strides and was virtually clinging onto the back of his rucksack. He assured her with a tight-lipped grin that it was okay and that it was just a large, six-foot long, yellow and black spotted jaguar. *Oh, that's okay then!* frets Katty. Sergio said the jaguar was only giving out a warning growl for them not to come any closer. Katty raised a quivering eyebrow. *Seriously? Sergio calling it a large cat. Really?* A jaguar cat is the size of a leopard, and it is not a fluffy, domestic pussy cat! *Here, pussy, pussy!* she imagines Sergio beckoning the jaguar to give it a playful pat on its friendly meowing head. *I don't think so!* she shudders. Katty stiffens her white knuckled grip tightly onto Sergio's rucksack. She doesn't feel fully assured of his explanation. Katty frets that she will have to get used to the non-domestic animals playing in their big back garden.

The hot and moist air clings around them like a hot, sweaty, quilted cloud. Their nostrils are filled with a thick stench of rotting leaves and a tangy strong, sweet flower scent. The birds and howler monkeys screech and howl from beneath the dense umbrella canopy overhead. Hidden ghostly creatures shuffle and scurry beneath the foliage, causing the ground to move as leaves rustle in their search among the forest floor for food. Insects skuttle, buzz and hum, and armies of ants yomp in line with military precision in quickstep stomping along leaves, branches and tree roots.

The clammy humidity meant Katty had to keep adjusting her sticky dark purple headband to keep her dangling fringe from draping over her eyes like a curtain. Mum gave Katty's fringe just a little trim. She could blink freely now and her blurry vision had vanished. The fringe was a little crooked and slanted,

Katty grumbled, but Mum ruffled her hair and would not admit to it, of course.

Katty stands still, slowly arching her neck to scan her surroundings. She can see a three-toed sloth clinging onto a tree. At first sight the sloth was seemingly motionless, swathed in green algae-infested fur which acts as camouflage from predators. But Katty can see that the sloth is lazily munching on the leaves, twigs and buds. That was so like Jake. Katty smirked as she imagined the sloth and Jake slothfully chomping food in a treehouse at home.

'Oh, look Jake,' points Katty to the side of a tree. Jake frowns and stares quizzically. 'The sloth and you must be related,' she chortles. 'It's got the same gormless smile as you.' She couldn't help but snort through her nose like a pig. Jake grunted something but Katty couldn't make it out.

She thinks it is a lucky thing the sloth is in disguise as just above the trees a giant harpy eagle menacingly soars in search for a favourite sloth meal. The eagle's gigantic sharp talons dangle frighteningly, just waiting to clamp onto its prey. The shriek of the harpy eagle slices through the air. Gulping throats. Trickling beads of sweat. Trembling bodies. The fear in the sloth's eyes was glistening, staring in the hope that the harpy eagle would not see him. The monkeys, sloths, macaws, iguanas and snakes slither, scramble and scurry for cover into the knucks and crannies of the trees and branches, quivering in fear, staring anxiously with bulbous eyes. They dare not take their eyes off the harpy eagle's flight. The three-foot tall harpy eagle is massive - nearly as tall as Jake. It weighs about one-and-a-half stone, like a ten-pin bowling ball, not to mention the harpy eagle's outstretched wingspan of six-and-a-half foot. Six-and-a-half foot! That is taller than Dad. Katty cannot see all the animals, but she can hear the trees are filled with a cacophony of sounds reverberating in the treetops with squawking trills of scarlet macaws and croaking, barking toucans.

CHAPTER 4

Seeing Double-Double

The humidity makes Katty's heart gallop as she sucks in pockets of muggy air. She squints towards the tops of the trees, way up high. The trees seem to be touching the clear blue sky and scorching, beaming sunrays dazzle. The heat pounds at her buzzing head. She can see a double vision of swirling, wavey, swaying, dancing trees. It is hot and she is drenched in sweat and her head feels light and giddy. She feels still and her head is floaty and dreamy. She blinks away the trickling perspiration puddling around her eyes and a blurry mirage of an ice cream van flickers and quivers in front of her. *No way*, her thoughts fuzzed. She'd never imagined having a ninety-nine ice cream in the middle of the jungle!

'Jake,' she whispers, raising a pointed finger. 'Jake. Look! It's Mr Fudge's ice cream van.'

Jake frowned. He sticks his tongue out to catch the waterfall of perspiration streaming down his face. It is unbearable. His neck and face prickled. Even in the sticky humidity he felt like his head was a bright orange flashing beacon perched on his shoulders warning the whole jungle of his presence. He couldn't see Mr Fudge or his ice cream van. *Katty must be sleepwalking or something*, he thought. Jake stopped unsteadily and turned to Mum, Dad and Sergio who were walking a short distance behind them.

'Mum, I'm feeling very hot,' croaked Jake, 'and Katty is acting all weird. She says she can see Mr Fudge's ice cream van. She must be seeing things.'

Sergio rushed over to Katty and ushered her and Jake to a shaded area in between the spider-legged roots of one of the ginormous trees. Sergio smiled a comforting smile. It was a reassuring smile for a dizzy, confused and disorientated Katty, even if she didn't realise it. Jake was right. Even Katty thought her blurry, wavery vision of an ice cream van was a bit weird.

'It is not normal for an ice cream van to show up in the middle of the rainforest,' chirps up Dad, talking more to Jake than anyone else. Jake smirked a weary, twitchy grin.

'You must drink lots of water or the heat will shrink your brain and you will start to see peculiar things,' instructed Sergio. Katty didn't like the idea of her brain shrinking as a glug of water rolled down her tongue to the back of her throat, then trickled down into her oesophagus and her stomach. She continued gulping down small gluggy sips to get her brain back to normal.

'Was she hallucinating?' Mum asked Sergio, wiping Katty's brow and gently patting her cheeks with a flannel. 'She's burning up a fever.'

'It's okay. It is normal for the body to adjust to the heat and humidity,' explains Sergio sympathetically. 'She just needs to drink plenty of water. Keep sipping the water every ten to fifteen minutes. That will be more than enough. Otherwise, she will be seeing Yetis next.'

Katty pressed her lips to give a pained grin and sipped some more water, one refreshing gulp at a time. She was already feeling a little cooler and now everything was a bit clearer and back in focus. The blurriness had gone, and so had Mr Fudge's ice cream van.

CHAPTER 5

Yeti Attack!

Trundling through the jungle Katty and Jake shuffle through the undergrowth in the wake of Mum, Dad and Sergio. Katty squinted and peered into the dense, white, sickly mist. Was it shapes she could see moving in the mist? Could she see flickering eyes blinking at her? A shiver rippled up her spine and she stiffened her shoulders. The mist did not seem to fade away, dissolve or lift. It just hung there, draped amongst the trees and branches like a spooky ghostly blanket. Lofty and Spike peer back at her through the mist with their brown bulging knotted eyes.

'I wish we would be left alone by the farmers, loggers and tourists,' croaks Spike, spitting out leaves.

'I dooz wish you would leaves *me* aloneses,' quips Lofty.

'Every tree I know would wish you to be left alone too!' grunts Spike with a snarled stare.

'Huh. Really?' Lofty pauses in a deep, wrinkly frown. 'Anyways. I thinks the little touristsy girl can sees and hears us too. Spooky, huh,' chuckles Lofty.

'I know how she feels. I have to put up with seeing and hearing you all the time. That's worse than spooky,' snorts Spike.

Katty still couldn't believe how tall the Kapok beanstalk-like trees were. The trees just seemed elasticated and stretched way up high into the sky. The Kapok tree stretched up like a skyscraper. Katty stepped over and in between the spider-like roots, heaving herself up and leaning up against the bark of the tree. She reached her arms out as far as she could to either side. To be able to hug and link arms to wrap around the tree it would take two of her, Jake, Sergio and Miss Violet put together. She could smell and sense the sap pulsing along its veins to the heartbeat of the bulky tree. Katty places the palm of her hand on the bark of the tree. She closes her eyes and transmits her thoughts down her arm, through the palm of her hand and into the tree's crinkly bark. She believes she is able to talk to Lofty or Spike, even if Lofty thought she is a *stupidsy* tourist and Spike had said tourists don't belong in the jungle. She didn't care. She just wanted them to know she was there for them.

Katty reckons they whisper mysterious tales of their past lives. There was a chorus of distant, echoey, whispering, raspy voices – sniggering, chuckling and teasing. The jungle was filled with superstitions about jungle spirits that live in the trees, ancient tribes, loggers, farmers, ranchers and even talking animals. Her whole body trembles as her legs turn all wibbly-wobbly and jelly-like. Proper spooky.

Sergio paces ahead in long strides. Katty and Jake quick march into a trot, pass the dawdling Mum and Dad, and shuffle alongside Sergio. They had to speed walk just to keep up with him.

Katty trudges alongside Sergio with Jake jabbering nonsense into his ear. Katty's eyes squint and flicker like a nervous meerkat on lookout patrol. She can't help but feel they are being followed and watched. She thought she caught glimpses of shiny, shimmering eyes stalking them. She supposed the eyes could belong to an elasticated, long-limbed spider monkey hanging upside down on a branch by one arm, smiling inquisitively and just passing the day away. *No. No*, she decided. The eyes didn't belong to smiley faces. But she sensed a chill in the hot, humid air and that made it feel more frightening. She imagined beady eyes belonging to a silky, shiny black-furred panther tracking their every movement, just waiting to pounce.

She smells danger, it chilled her bones. It felt creepy and scary. She couldn't shake off the piercing eeriness, the laser beam-like stares. These were typical of hungry skulking salivating predators, she imagined. And that meant trouble. She gulped. Her whole body shuddered, prickling her sweaty, clammy skin. Beady eyes with disguised invisible bodies scanning their prey. *Oh crikey*, she realises. She is the prey, and she is being stalked and hunted. Her chest heaves out a gasp. Jake turns around with a tut and a frown. Katty scowls back at him. She is on an expedition, and she doesn't like the idea of being hunted as prey. Sergio held up his hand in an abrupt stop.

'Stop walking,' whispers Sergio, as he crouches down and peers through his binoculars. Mum and Dad look at each other, eyebrows raised. Jake froze and stared wide-eyed at the back of Sergio's head, waiting for further instructions. Katty raises on her tiptoes to get a better vantage point, about 100 millimetres higher. But still, she could see nothing, and especially without her own binoculars. A vacuum of air was sucked in and each one of them held their breath. Beads of sweat trickled and rolled down Katty's forehead, goosebumps prickled her spine. *What next?* she frets. She dares not even shake her head in despair. A light distant rumble gently vibrates beneath their feet. It was like something from Jurassic Park as if the dinosaurs were descending upon them. *Strange*, thinks Katty. *Very strange.* The ground begins to shake and pound like a murmuring tremor. She looks to the ground beneath her mud strewn trekking boots. Her eyes peek up to the sound of swish-crackling rustles in the near distance and whatever it was seemed to be approaching right in the direction to where she stood. It was certainly coming right towards them at a quick pace. Her heart pounds so hard she could feel her ribs twang and her head pulsed a thronging pain.

'Run,' bellows Sergio. 'Get out of here. Hurry!' They all turn on their toes and scarper, rapidly scurrying through the undergrowth. The rustling vegetation and crackling branches behind them are getter louder and louder, closer and closer. Katty doesn't know whether it's a large black panther or black speckled yellow jaguar charging at them. *Crikey!* It could be a gang of loggers with guns or a hunting tribe with bows, arrows and spears. Katty's head pounds in shear panic. She can't believe she is being hunted. Her heart skitters like bouncing on a rickety trampoline and she could feel the fear surging and rumbling into knots in her stomach, ready to fray and explode. Five pairs of bulging eyes scream in horror! Five humans pelt it as fast as their legs can carry them. They are all in complete terrifying fear and trembling despair. Then the loud pounding rustling noise disperses into nothing just as quickly into what

Katty hoped was in another direction and away from her. Katty's leg muscles and lungs burned of starved oxygen. Her legs felt like jelly and her lungs like the inside of a blazing, intense oven on gas mark ten. That's two hundred and sixty degrees Celsius… very, very hot. Placing her hands on her knees she heaved her chest up and down, gasping for a meaningful intake of air. She heaved and gasped heavily. Her body quivered in the adrenaline rush of flight to survive. If only she could fly, she wished. She wanted to cry in relief.

'It's gone,' pants Sergio. 'Whatever it was, it's gone.'

'What is it?' pleads Katty, looking at Sergio with wide, petrified eyes.

'It might have been a jaguar chasing a deer or capybara or something. It's okay for now. It's safe.'

'Okay for now? What do you mean, okay for now?' pleads Mum, wheezing and frantically sucking in gulps of oxygen as Dad held her upright. *She must have had the wobbly legs thing too*, Katty supposed. Jake looks as if he is okay, but he was doing a slanted forced grin, trying to hide the terror of the last thirty seconds. His face white ashen, Sergio puffs out a lungful of air. He pants a nervous laugh with his eyes darting around for any sign of movement. The tension in the air crackles around them. They are on tenterhooks, nervously looking at each other. The feeling of relief hung in the air.

The walk back to camp was quiet of chit-chat as their quick shuffling feet marched them on with great relief. Sergio had told them of the Brazilian Amazon Yeti. A large, red-furred bear-sized Yeti that wanders through the rainforest. Katty gulped.

'Could that have been the rumbling predator we just ran from?' asks Katty with squinted eyes.

'It could have been anything,' lies Sergio. There had been many sightings of the Yeti over the years, and he had no reason to doubt the witnesses.

Katty and Jake couldn't get back to the campsite quick enough as they scurried into the cabins and collapse onto their beds, hoping not to encounter that 'whatever-it-was' *thing* again. It was just an innocent animal chasing another or something like that, suggested Sergio. Katty reflected and seriously wondered, chillingly, if it was the giant, furry Yeti. She puffs her cheeks out, exhaling her relief. Her heart rate was back to normal, and she felt a lot more chilled about the whole event now. Her tummy rumbles. She looks forward to dinner. *What could possibly be on the menu today?* she ponders. *Mmmm! Yummy!* She hopes the grilled tiger catfish wrapped in a luscious green leaf was an option on the kitchen menu for today. She didn't even mind the thin layer of her five-a-day vegetables of onions, tomatoes, chillies and coriander sat on top of the sizzling fish. Katty's nostrils tingle and twitch. Whiffs of twirling puffs of steam rise from the scrumptious tucupi sweet, salty, yellow sauce. She rolls her lips. It was definitely a 'yummy' mouth dribbling, salivating moment. *What would the Yeti eat? Ah, yes. Mmmm*, she muses. *Curly twigs, branches and tree bark dipped in dung. Yuk!* That might be yummy for a Yeti.

The early evening sprinkles the dimming, dazzling speckles of the sunset dusk. Whispers echo in the light, swirling warm breeze. The murmurs of the forest call out the nocturnal animals, insects, grubs and creepy crawlies into the forest and Katty's campsite. She thought of Spike and Lofty. They were arguing again. She senses their tension in the air.

You always knew when Spike was angry. The sap starts to seep through his bark, bubbling slowly into a gurgling simmer. The simmering bubbles gurgle louder as he gets angrier, and he gets more irritated because that's what he does. Lofty always gets under his bark and Spike's cracked bark leaks the sap bubbling gurgles even more. The pleasant, rosy smell of the sap lingers in the air like a spray of deodorant. The sweet, rosy smell belongs to Spike; the lingering sickly scent confirms to Lofty that Spike needs anger management classes. Lofty gives Spike a bark-splitting smirk. Spike scowls a knotty grimace.

Katty wonders if the rustling branch whisperings were Spike and Lofty bickering yet again. Maybe they were trying to warn her of looming danger. Her eyes flicker and dart all around for any sign of movement or lurking, staring beady eyes. She was all too aware by now of the dangers, like a stampeding Yeti. She shudders. Jaguars, alligators, piranha fish. There were more dangers than she could think of. She gulps.

Katty changes out of her big clunky boots, peels off her stinking socks, and slips into a pair of sparkly pink slip-on trainers. She was glad to be out of her stinking mud-clad boots. Her feet had squelched in the boggy mud in her sodden socks. If only she could levitate out of the mud, she mused, better still if she could levitate all the way up to the top of the trees like a drone. That would be awesome. She could see Sergio fiddling about with some camera equipment that had been attached to a drone. She stepped down from the cabin porch and sidled up alongside him and Jake to view Sergio's camera screen.

Sergio shows Katty and Jake some drone footage above the canopy. They can see the lush treetops with rustling leaves where monkeys are swinging and jumping amongst the high branches. Katty's eyes glisten in awe. If only she could fly like a giant, harpy eagle. She could be gliding and swooning, witnessing the undulating green waves of the rainforest canopy. As the drone flew further afield Katty could see smouldering smoke and toothless gaps of flattened lands. She noticed that the bare land areas have been scorched by fire and there were other areas that had been cleared of trees for timber. Sergio explained the areas had been cleared for farming. The land could be used for growing crops, or it could also be for cattle ranching for beef.

'What do you mean by beef, Sergio?' asked Jake. 'I don't get it.' Katty looked at Sergio with raised eyebrows and turned to frown at Jake and roll her eyes.

'O-o-k-kay,' stammered Jake, squinting his eyes full of suspicion. Had he missed something so obvious for Katty to roll her eyes in that patronising manner? She could be so full of herself sometimes; it made his blood boil.

'How can one so little be so thick?' she blurted scoffingly. 'Beef burgers. Duh!'

'I know that. I'm not thick, stupid,' snapped Jake. He scowled at Katty then turned to Sergio, who put his palms up, resigned himself to calm things down and he gently nodded.

'Okay,' he said with a dimpled grin. Jake and Katty sensed a lecture coming on. Sergio ignored their sighs and droopy rolling eyes.

'Latin America is one of the largest exporters of beef on the planet and this land is being chopped, burned and bulldozed for the sake of humans wanting to eat more and more steak, and more and more burgers,' exclaimed Sergio. 'The world only seems to want to eat more and more meat. More meat means more cattle; more cattle mean less trees. We must all eat less meat. There are other foods, you know,' said Sergio in a resigned tone. He even looked fed up and deflated at the thought of knowing that a third of all food in the world is wasted through buying more than is needed; overstocking shelves and expiring shelf lives.

A third of all food is thrown away. He shook his head. Mindboggling, he fumed. And yet people starve and live in food poverty. Sergio frowned and churned the thoughts in his mind. He could never figure it out.

It perplexes Katty. Her forehead wrinkles as she works it out in her mind. *So, the farmers and ranchers chop down trees to grow crops and feed cattle. Cattle means deforestation. It's as simple as that,* she fumed. That message had to get out there, people had a right to know. Beef means deforestation. It also meant destroying the habitat of already endangered species like the 'lazy bear' sloth.

'Oh my gosh,' gasps Katty. This is proper 'Fact of the Day' stuff for their Climate Summit meeting, and it was on a mega, massive scale. Cattle ranching for red meat makes up eighty per cent of deforestation. That's mega scary and mega bad news too.

CHAPTER 6

Clickety-clack, clickety-clack

Katty had slept well and was pleased she had survived another bite-free night from the pesky mosquitoes. Today was a special trip day and it didn't involve stomping around too much. She had a spring in her step after breakfast. *Yippee!* she shudders excitedly. She was about to go on a riverboat ride along the famous Amazon river. She didn't mind water as she could swim at least two widths of a swimming pool with only having to breathe once. But she had no intention of swimming in this river because she didn't fancy being eaten by jaw-clenching alligators or eaten by jaw-munching piranha fish. *Uh-uh*. She definitely wasn't swimming. And that was that. She would keep her arms folded tightly around the life jacket.

The riverboat was moored up near the river embankment alongside the small, walking pier. She trundled along the wooden planks of the pier and stepped over the yellow-painted upper edge gunwale of the side of the boat and into the riverboat. It rocked gently on its green hull. Its green wooden canopy was tall enough for her to easily stand underneath as she stepped onto the wooden, slatted seats. She sat down in the front end of the boat's bow. The riverboat swayed gently as Katty huddled under the green canopy roof and Jake clumsily tumbled into the riverboat too. Mum and Dad squeezed in behind her. Katty huffed as she had to contend with being next to the little fidgety worm, Jake.

Jake began jabbering on about how they could do a spot of piranha fishing along the way. *Are you mad?* thought Katty in utter disbelief at what the idiot, Jake, was spouting off about. *Seriously? Really?* she huffed and shook her head to no one in particular. No way would she be fishing for piranhas. The piranhas have ferocious sharp gnashers and can devour its prey in a frenzied flesh eating attack in just a matter of minutes, leaving only the skeletal bones behind. *Uh-uh. Not happening; not a chance.* A cold chill shuddered up her spine. She sat upright, looking straight ahead with folded arms over her life jacket to make sure her hands stayed well inside the riverboat. Jake could fish for piranhas if he wanted to, of course, but no way was she doing it. The riverboat's outboard engine at the rear of the boat was thrust into life and momentarily coughed and spluttered out puffs of blue smoke. The ponytailed pilot twisted the throttle and the riverboat chugged into a jerky, stuttering plod making its way clear of the jetty. They were off. The riverboat straightens up and reaches out into the long stretch of river ahead. Katty faces forward and grins to herself in excited anticipation of the unknown adventure that awaits her. Her heartbeat picked up from a slow steady walk into an invigorating, lively trot. Clip-clop, clip-clop, clip-clop, her heart trotted merrily. She couldn't stop smiling. Jake might think she had gone mad with her fixed smile on her face. It might look like a demented, weird, crazy smile.

But she didn't care. The journey ahead felt like Christmas Day –unwrapping an unknown surprise gift without knowing who bought it.

What would it be like meeting the tribe? she wondered. It felt surreal, like how could it even be possible. She felt a bit tense with a tinge of panic as her nerves burnt right through her body. Her bones quivered and she shuddered under the life jacket. A course of adrenaline rushed into her bloodstream and her whole persona spiked at the thought of going out on this adventure. Excitement, yes, and there could be danger too. She enthused with as much confidence as she could muster, a mixture of excitement and fear as she fidgeted and twirled the ends of her hair with her fingers. It didn't seem real, but she was actually going to mingle with an indigenous tribe. And if that wasn't exciting enough, she might even get to feed pink dolphins. Her head sparkled; her face beamed. She was so thrilled that she did a little shoulder shimmy.

Sergio stood alongside the tall, gangly pilot. They were yapping away and pointing at the animals along the riverbanks. Katty supposed the pilot could see in all directions like that of an owl's swivelling head. He was so tall he could even see above the canopy roof as they trundled along. She looked over her shoulder to see Mum and Dad smiling at her. She smiles back and turns to face the front of the boat and watched the wonders of the lush green forest. The boat chugs along the silky smooth, calm Amazon river, churning up small tidal ripples in the wake of the riverboat's murmuring, spluttering engine.

The tourist riverboat waddles and sways its green hull merrily along the contours of the wide snaking, winding and twisty river. Katty breathed in the tranquillity and peace of the overhanging green trees as their shadows reflect on the river's mirror-like surface. The trees harbour a vast array of exotic, tropical animal life. She could hear the birds happily twittering, whistling and chirping as well as the parrots clicking their tongues to trill and purr. She smiles in bliss. In the distance Katty thinks she can make out monkeys barking in gravelly, grunting honks. She glances to her right as the monkeys remind her of Jake; she smirked inside.

Katty didn't know if she was awake or dreaming, whether minutes or hours had passed by. It was sheer bliss. The rippling, rushing water whooshed and gurgled serenely in the wake of the riverboat's light gargling grunts and the odd puff of blue smoke. The sounds and bright colours reminded her of Rivendell, Middle Earth in *The Lord of the Rings*. She was the magical, majestic elf, Lady Galadriel. This was how she felt floating on the aura of the Amazon river. In her daydream land she was on an adventure seeking out The Goblin King and running away from the Orcs. If that wasn't enough, she had to take charge of Gollom - her little annoying brother, Jake. He sat next to her on the riverboat. He was oblivious to his Gollom status. She imagined he would just shrug his shoulders at being called Gollom. He was her prisoner. Katty's (Lady Galadriel's) powers were to protect and preserve. She decided she held the power to protect Jake from the piranhas. Katty smirks as she remembered that Lady Galadriel also had mind reading powers. *Spooky, huh*. Mind reading powers... just like Mum did with her telepathic powers too. Katty closed her eyes to savour the aura as she sucks in a lungful of Amazonian air and exhales lazily through her nose. It was a yoga technique she and Mum did loads of times in the garage at home. It was their space to practice their zen yoga and flexi-bendy aerobics, away from Dad and Jake.

The river gushes and gurgles as the currents ripple along the river. Jake peers into the flowing river with insects and flies dancing across the surface. It seems a little cooler on the river. His glance turns into a stare. Katty knows he's gone into one – a world of his own. She presses her lips and frowns. *Pity. He's lost in his own thoughts.* Jake wonders where the river starts and ends. He'd heard about big dams being built. What does it mean to break the path of the river? he had asked Sergio. Flooding, that's what Sergio had mentioned. The dams create reservoirs by holding the water, raising the water levels, and drowning the trees, causing them to rot and belch out pollutants into the atmosphere.

Jake turns around on his bench and looks to Mum.

'Mum, Sergio says there are dams on the river. To stop Dad stealing your brick-sized chocolate brownies, you could use them to build the dams,' jokes Jake with a beaming smile. The grin on Jake's face pushes his cheeks up high. He was chuffed at the cleverness of his reference to Mum's brick-sized brownies. Mum's eyes open wide in disbelief. Dad coughs a laugh and feigns disbelief, shaking his head with a deep knitted frown – firmly in Jake's direction. Mum looks from Jake to Dad and back to Jake again. Jake twitches an apologetic grin. He mouths 'sorry' and bows his head to avert Mum's laser steely stare.

'Tut, tut, tut,' mutters Mum.

Katty smiles on the inside and fakes a frown of disgust.

'Yeah. Tut, tut, tut,' mutters Katty, smarmily. 'Show some respect to your elders, Jake. Mum could be on the telly in MasterChef. That's what I reckon.' Jake wouldn't dare respond nastily to that; she knew. Her eyes twinkle. Mummy's boy has just lost some brick-sized brownie points. *Pardon the pun.* She smirks.

Katty dozily slunk out of her daydream. Weariness was beginning to set in. Jake still jabbered on about stupid stuff. No change there, then. Chitter-chatter mutterings reverberated in and around the wooden-slatted seats behind her, but she didn't want to turn around just in case someone spoke to her. She blinks and gazes straight ahead. There was another bend to the right coming up in the river and the ponytail pilot gradually leaned the tiller to the left to steer the boat's rudder. The gentle rippling surface of the river glistened with the sun's reflection and the riverboat slunk forward to the gentle stuttering, wheezing hum of the outboard engine. The riverboat veered around the bend and straightened up again with the tiller in the centre position. Katty noticed small breaks in the river's surface. They were like little plops and trickles of disturbance from something beneath the surface. She leaned forward instinctively, squinting her eyes for a closer inspection. What could it be? She hoped they weren't piranhas searching for human fleshy meat, she winced. *Didn't alligators come near the surface when searching for prey?* She was about to nudge Jake when all of a sudden...

'Woah! What's that?' Katty squealed, pointing her hand in the direction of plonking splashes in what looked like bobbing heads poking in and out of the water. *Yes, there were certainly bobbing heads of something, more than one, possibly three or four,* she enthused. *Whoosh!* A large fish leaps out of the water in an arc motion, splashing back into a dive. A cacophony of raucous, echoey crackling clicks and ringing whistles reverberate from the water.

'Pink dolphins,' shouted the ponytail man. 'Just ahead. We'll moor up on the riverbank and see if we can entice them with some food.' He turned off the throttle with a twist of his hand. The engine spluttered and coughed and then went silent. He had shut the engine off and the riverboat coasted slowly, and the ponytail man steered towards the side of the river to a nearby bank to moor up.

The small pod of pink dolphins clicked, clacked and whistled excitedly. The cacophony of clicks, clacks and whistles echoed across the river.

Mum, Dad, Jake and Katty gingerly stepped over the wooden-slatted seats and shuffle along to spread out and reach over the yellow-trimmed gunwale towards the pink dolphins. The inquisitive pink dolphins come up to the surface. First comes their long beaks protruding the water, followed by a prominent domed forehead with small eyes. Katty thought they looked like they were constantly smiling. Their beaks nattered in eagerness to clamp onto the fish bait. The ponytail man held out a litter grabber which was holding a fish to feed the dolphins. As the dolphins 'stood' out of the water with their flapping flippers to nab a fish, Katty could reach out and touch their smooth, soft, silky bodies. *Wow!* A fuzzy jolt of joy whizzed through her body. *Cool,* she buzzed. Her eyes remained transfixed at the bobbing heads of pink dolphins. She couldn't help but smile.

Ponytail man stepped over the gunwale onto the riverbank and waded through the shallow water to be in amongst the pink dolphins. The water was only up to his waist. With a nervous approving nod from Mum and Dad and a reassuring pat on their shoulders, Katty and Jake are lifted out of the boat by ponytail man and carefully plonked either side of the tall pilot whilst he continued to feed the dolphins with the fish pincered between his index finger and thumb at his shoulder height. It was a shock but so cool. The funny-looking pink dolphins were so tame. Mum's mouth flopped open in surprise; Dad just grinned, his eyes beaming in awe.

Sergio nods with a tight-lipped grin and says that they are honoured to be in the presence of the river 'pink' dolphins as they are under threat of extinction because of pollution.

'Pollution?' probes Katty. Her voice squeals in her surprise.

'Yes. Pollution seeps into the rivers all the time. Murky red mercury trickles into the rivers from leaking mineworks and there are drills going deep into the ground for oil and gas. Chemicals from farming spills enter the rivers too. The dolphins are even poached to be used as bait for fishing,' exclaims Sergio, shaking his head, 'because the dolphins are seen as competition to the fishermen for fish.'

'That's cruel,' croaks Katty. She didn't mean it to be so loud, but she was vexed at the fishermen killing the dolphins to use for bait. A splash of water from the dolphins distracts Katty's sad thoughts.

Jake's face smirks a twisted grin as he watches ponytail man feed the dolphins. Sergio notices bubbles coming from under the water. He frowns, purses his lips, and cocks his head to one side as he stares at the surface of the water near Jake.

'What are those bubbles from under the water?' points Sergio.

Jake frowned in protest of his innocence to Sergio. Jake's mind hums in protest.

'Okay, Sergio,' murmurs Jake. 'No need to make a fuss.'

'Bubbles from where? Are they bubbles?' utters Sergio in a deep frown. 'No. That can't be right, can it?'

Sergio continues to point close to where Jake was stood. *Okay, maybe they are bubbles*, Jake concedes. His cheeks prickle to a light shade of red.

'Bubbles? What bubbles?' smirks Jake, raising his eyebrows. Katty knew straight away what the bubbles were all about. The dirty, disgusting, stinky worm. *Unbelievable!* chides Katty. As if there wasn't enough pollution in the river already. There were definitely bubbles. Sergio knew it; Katty knew it; Jake knew it; the bubbles knew it! The bubbles. It was Jake. He was farting under the water.

Jake giggles to himself when he farts. Mum's laser glare puts a stop to that. His cheeks blush scarlet red because he'd been caught. Dad went to do a high-five with Jake and immediately thought better of it. Instead, he decided to give Jake a naughty boy Dad frown. *Thanks Dad!* fretted Jake in thought. Jake was gutted and still trapped in Mum's laser stare. He was waiting for the telepathic connection from Mum to give him a right telling off.

'It was an accident, Mum. I didn't mean it. It's Dad's fault. He gave me dodgy apricots earlier,' pleaded Jake with puppy dog eyes, managing to point a limp index finger in the direction of Dad.

Mum gave Dad a glancing, disapproving look. Dad raised his eyebrows in innocence to Mum and then gave Jake a retorting '*you little rat*' scowl. Jake offered a sorry dimpled grin. Katty was very happy. *Yippee!* She was definitely Mum and Dad's favourite child now.

Feeding the pink dolphins had been awesome, trilled Katty's mind. Jake was keeping schtum after his farting antics and Mum's disapproving laser beam glare. Katty was glad of the little worm's silence of guilt. She was still excited. They would be at the tribal camp soon as the riverboat chugged merrily along the bendy river.

CHAPTER 7

Feather Me Down!

The riverboat coughs and splutters to a gliding halt as it tilts and leans into the sloping green embankment. They gingerly disembark, stepping over the boat's gunwale and onto dry land. A snaking pathway meanders up to the edge of the village. Katty could see lots of huts at the top of the riverbank, and she could see Sergio traipsing jauntily with a bouncy spring in his step further into the indigenous tribe's camp. He smiled and ruffled the little toddlers' hair as they scurried excitedly around him. He tiptoed and ducked his head under a shaded bamboo canopy with its high thatched roof. Sergio disappeared into a large hut.

Katty, excitedly, curiously and sheepishly stepped forward through the small, buzzing, cackling settlement of a tribal village. She passed the open fires burning sweet sap and weaved her way through the overhanging canopies until she too arrived at the large open-spaced hut. She was fizzling like a bottle of pop with nervous energy, her toes tingling and butterflies fluttering in his chest. She stepped inside.

There were benches laid out against the hut walls, and the walls were decorated with indigenous colourful tribal paintings of mixed shapes and designs. It was like an art gallery. The paintings were brightly coloured and eye-catching, admired Katty.

An old man caught Katty's attention. The old man reminded her of Gramps. He was a proper tribesman. His face partially painted with squiggly lines across his forehead and cheeks, and a dotted line along the bridge of his nose. Sergio had mentioned tribal face paintings had important meanings. Katty knew it wasn't anything to do with Halloween. There were different face paint markings, she knew, for religious ceremonies, hunting, war, beauty and good fortune, but she couldn't tell which was which. They all looked so different to her at any rate.

Katty reckoned Jake would have Super Mario super mushrooms painted on his cheeks and she decided she would have a tree painted on each cheek too. On one cheek she would have a tree for Spike and on the other cheek a tree for Lofty. She caught Jake's eye gazing in a frown around the hut. Typical, she mused. He was probably wondering where the Mario Kart gaming station and big screen were.

Katty couldn't help it, the further she walked into the hut, the further her jaw dropped ajar. She was aghast. The hut was massive. *Wow!* It was awesome. It was like going back in time. The old man had a big, broad beaming smile. Perched on top of his head was a crown headband adorned with colourful blue, green and yellow feathers and he wore a beautiful necklace made of jaguar teeth. Her insides quaked. Quite how he obtained the jaguar teeth Katty didn't care to consider.

She spotted he was wearing swimming trunks covered with a piece of painted fabric hanging down the front and a large forest leaf on the back. They all wore beautiful necklaces made of seeds, feathers and shells. Their faces were painted in squiggly lines, dashes and dots in all varieties of patterns. The men had awesome feathered crowns and the women wore long, dangly feathered earrings that draped down to their waists.

'Oh!' gasps Katty, quickly placing a hand over her mouth. They women weren't wearing anything above their waists to cover their tops apart from the dangly, feathered earrings draping down their fronts. *Oh, flippity-flip!* She could see the women's boobs. Jake's face peached and he looked over his shoulder to Mum. Katty frowns, presses her lips tight and looks towards Mum too for some sort of explanation or disapproval, knowing Mum's opinions on all things dress code... or lack of a dress or a bra.

'Why are their boobs not covered up, Mum?' whispers Jake. His eyes scrunched up. Mum placed her hand on his shoulder and whispered into his ear.

'It's their tradition. It's normal to them so don't stare or pull funny faces, please. Good boy.' Katty could hear Mum's warning to Jake, so she decided to add her own warning.

'Or don't you dare fart either!' quips Katty smugly. Mum's steely glare slaps away Katty's smug grin. *Ouch!* Jake raises his eyebrows that lifts his cheeks. He is the one with a smug smile now.

Katty, Jake, Sergio, Mum and Dad robotically shuffled their feet along the ground inside the traditional thatched-roof hut. Their shuffling feet made their way across to the outer inside perimeter of the hut and they quietly sat down. They were joined a few minutes later by the tribesmen, tribeswomen and little tribal children. Katty briefly darted her eyes to the busy throng of bench dwellers and then stared ahead and waited pensively for the show to start. She didn't have to wait long. No sooner had she had settled down the tribal old man yodels out words. His words ring around the inside of the hut. He is welcoming them to their home. Katty had no clue what he had said.

Suddenly, the seated tribal women, men and children jump to their feet, playing maracas and percussion instruments as they chant tribal songs. The atmosphere was charged with vigour and joy like an aurora sparkling in the air. Some of the women beckon them to join in the dance. Mum and Dad spring up and intertwine their arms. Katty stays rigid to her seat, beaming inside at the marvel of the animal-hunting mimicry dance. It was no Taylor Swift concert, but the same magic and energy sparkled in the air. One tribesman, dressed in long draping strands of plaited straw from his shoulders to his knees, was banging a tin drum with a stick whilst walking in dizzying circles. Other tribesmen wore feathered hats and played flutes that sounded like gasping, whinging bagpipes. The women and children danced with arms interlinked and in quick steps, they jutted forward, sprung back and skipped around the large hut's fancy, designed multi-coloured poles.

Katty and Jake wonder if the spiritual leader could give them tips on how to ward off demonic spirits. They thought of a few things they would like to *not* have to do. Things like no more homework, no more being grounded, no more chores like cleaning bedrooms, tidying up or washing dishes. They chuckle and mimic as they recite each chore, and each misdemeanour Mum and Dad gave them. If they weren't careful the Mystrees might cast a spell on them for being so cheeky.

Katty slowly trundles her feet forward as she makes her way out of the hut. She notices a small stall outside. She is excited. The stall is littered with tribal gifts and jewellery items. Mum gives Katty and Jake 100 Brazilian real, that's about sixteen pounds each, to spend in the tribal village. The money helps the tribes to survive. Jake grins and darts to one of the few stalls at lightning speed. He points eagerly at the hanging item behind the young smiling lady and hands over a ten dollar bill. Jake turns to Mum and beams a wide smile. Mum is startled. Jake grins again beneath his newly acquired tribal face-painted mask. His eyes beam through the slots for eyeholes. It had a pointy nose, a wide toothy smile and was decorated with multicoloured squiggly lines. It reminded Mum of a spooky clown. Mum smirks and rolls her eyes.

Katty scours the tabletop for inspiration and then she sees it. It is a charming black, smooth, flat circular onyx stone with a hole through the middle. Her fingers scramble inside her pocket and she shuffles out a crispy ten dollar bill. She reaches her hand over to the old lady who smiles with sparkling eyes.

'Es bueno!' the old lady croons in a broad warm smile. The old lady's sweet, kind tone makes Katty beam inside.

'Gracias,' replies Katty meekly with a grateful nod of her head. Katty steps away from the stall and stands still. She can't take her eyes off the onyx stone as she twirls it in between her fingers. It was silky smooth and soothing. She is transfixed. An onyx stone offers protection and good luck. She could feel its inner strength. *Aah!* She had an idea. She parted with another five dollars of Mum's money and paid for a black, leather string necklace.

By inserting a loop of the leather string through the hole in the onyx stone, Katty then threads the ends of the leather string through the loop to secure the onyx stone. She twists the loose ends of the string together between her fingers and ties a knot. She now has her own personal necklace. It was her special 'good luck' charm necklace. It was her personal connection with the Amazon rainforest. She quickly loops it over her head and tucks it beneath her light coloured, maroon polar neck top. She smooths the stone pendant through her top. To her, it was a good luck charm and represents hope. She needs plenty of hope, but she realises that without hope she has nothing.

Nothing is not an option; hope is everything.

The eventful hours drew a jampacked day to a yawning weary end as the green, rickety riverboat chugs back to camp. Katty's head spins in heavenly delight filled with bliss. Her happy thoughts transmit to her happy, smiling face as she thinks back to the journey along the endless, peaceful, idyllic and mesmerising beauty of the Amazon river. Memories came flooding back when she had been feeding the pink dolphins and she had now been mingling with a real Amazon tribe. How cool was that? She was a little sad that the day had to finish but she was definitely happy to have witnessed some of the wonders of the Amazon river, even if Jake had contaminated the water with his disgusting farts.

Another moonset gleaned, streaming through the thicket of trees. Katty sighed wearily. She softly rubbed her droopy eyes. Time for bed. Mosquito spray – *check*, mosquito netting – *check*, switch the eco-air cooler on – *check*. Now it would be safe to go to sleep! The adrenaline has seeped away, her eyes ached to go into temporary shutdown and sleep recovery mode. Fatigue had set into Katty's body as she slumped and tucked herself into her overnight eco-cabin bed. She was overloaded with pent-up emotional excitement from the day's events. Her eyelids flickered as the images of feeding the pink dolphins and the visit to the tribe's camp came flooding back. She couldn't think of anything being able to top that level of excitement but knew tomorrow would be another day of thrills. Tomorrow was a visit to the Iguazu Falls, known as one of the natural wonders of the world. And she would be there to experience it and savour its wondrousness. Butterflies fluttered in her chest. Her eyes drooped closed, and she smiled meekly. Sleep swept her away into the night.

CHAPTER 8

Carpet Of Bones

The orange misty sunrise fills the sky. Sunrays stream and pierce through the skyscraper-forest canopy of the lanky trees. The sunbeams warm the air. Splays of golden green and brown ricochet down through the trees, bouncing and decorating the bark and branches and splashing down onto the spindly tree roots and grass. The forest illuminates the beautiful radiance of ancient untouched animals, known as fauna, and plants, known as flora. These wonderful fauna and flora make up the special ecosystem that is the world famous Amazon rainforest. Katty likens the rainforest to a beaming colourful oasis. And there are people tribes too, Katty enthused, with some tribes not ever having been in contact with other humans. *Spooky!* She eagerly awaits this adventure. An adventure sure to be filled with mystery and wonderment.

The dawn light speckles through the curtains into Katty's campsite cabin. She steps outside onto the porch and stands on the cabin steps leaning on the wooden balustrade, smiling, and looking aimlessly at the river and surrounding lanky tall trees. The light reflects and bounces off the glimmering surface of the river as dragonflies flitter and hover above the surface of the water. Bubbles of plonking, bobbing fish plop up and down. The surface of the river ripples, feathering out into a calm tranquil flatness.

It is another morning filled with rustling undergrowth around the edges of the campsite. The birds chirp and squawk. Monkeys screech and scream high up into the distant tree canopy above.

Katty drumrolls her fingers on top of the railing of the cabin porch steps. She huffs a sigh. Her mind questions, her brow frowns. *Why can't these powerful world leaders put the climate as their number one priority?* It is affecting every country all around the world. Miss Violet says, 'you only have to look at the news and weather headlines in any country to see flooding, wildfires, drought, hunger, famine, poverty, air pollution; on and on and on and on.' Katty knew Miss Violet was right. *What more proof do they need? These leaders are always in competition to have bigger armies and exploring planets in space like Mars.* Katty exhales a deep breath. *If only they could stop being power-hungry politicians and join together to protect an earth that should not be overheating. Be chilled, live cool on a cooler planet.* Maybe she would use that as a campaign slogan. She'd bring it up at the next Climate Summit meeting. She grins. Jake will be jealous he didn't think of it first.

Mum, Dad, Katty and Jake shuffle into the breakfast cabin which offers an variety of yummy breakfast snacks. It was nothing like being at home in Redditch hustling in and around the kitchen table. It was always chaotic scrambling for toast, cereals and orange juice during breakfast time. The Amazon breakfast had a few surprises every day. Jake's favourite was the cheese and ham stuffed inside the bread and grilled to make a sandwich. This morning, there was something called Cassava, described as Brazilian Tapioca pancakes. The pancakes were folded neatly over banana slices on a thick gooey, yummy, scrumptious, slavering layer of chocolate spread. *Drip, drip, dribble. Dribble-eee-licious!* Much better than Mum's chocolate brownies, but nobody was ever going to mention that. The best breakfast ever.

'Bom dia,' gestures Sergio a good morning as he joyfully skipped into the breakfast area dodging in between the table and chairs and peering over the buffet serving of bananas, syrup, orange juice and a pot of coffee. The aromas were fresh, spritely, and enticing, supposed Katty. It certainly put a smile on her face. Her rumbling tummy is hushed, and she has a jumpy bouncy spring and a skip in her step.

'Olá fofa Katty and fofo Jake,' quips Sergio. Fofa and fofo was Sergio's way of saying cute kiddies or something like that.

'It is good to see you eating the local cuisine,' said Sergio with a nod and a sense of pride in the Brazilian array of food offerings.

'Olá fofo to you too, Sergio,' replied Jake. Sergio gave a grateful lopsided grin.

'Olá Senhora Sheehan. Olá Senor Sheehan.' Mum and Dad smiled at Sergio and then towards each other.

'Olá Senhora Sheehan,' quips Jake, immediately regretting it as Mum's stern, narrowed eyes gave him cause for concern. Katty's jaw dropped. *Oh, oh.* She knew Jake had absolutely overstepped the mark. He had no respect for his elders... including her.

'Just joking, Mum,' pipes up Jake sheepishly. 'Olá Mum. Your favourite child loves you!'

'I don't have a favourite child, Jake,' retorts Mum gruffly. Dad smirks and raises his eyebrows as he chews on a thick slab of toast. He wasn't going to get involved. Jake wasn't convinced about him not being Mum's favourite child because he was undeniably the cute one or as Sergio would say, 'fofo'. Yes, he was without doubt the cute, adorable younger sibling. And, as far as he was concerned, he was definitely the obvious choice to be favourite. End of story!

'Oh, come on Mum. We don't have to tell Katty I'm your favourite child,' he said. Katty's ears prick up at the mention of her name. She frowns. Her eyes dart from Mum to Jake then to Dad and then back to Mum.

'Tell Katty what, Mum?' interrupts Katty.

Mum tutted sarcastically and grinned.

'The "what" is that I don't have to tell you and Jake how much I love the pair of you,' Mum said, flicking a loving glance at Katty then at Jake. 'With no more love given to one of you any more than the other. Even if it doesn't always seem that way when you are playing up. But just the two of you, so don't tell your father,' instructs Mum with an agreeable wink and a nod. Jake smiles a beaming, chuffed smile. Katty gave Mum a confused half-grin not really knowing what she had heard or hadn't heard.

'Don't tell your father what?' Dad piped up curiously with a slanted grin. Senhora Sheehan huffed a feigned mocking, sinking sigh. She gave a cheeky smile. Katty and Jake chuckled.

'Never mind,' said Mum. 'Come on, you lot. Let's get breakfast finished and slap on that sun cream. Cover up please before the mozzies eat us alive.'

Splash, dash, slobber.

Another big dollop of sun cream is blobbed and smeared across the disgruntled faces of Katty and Jake by Mum.

The planned trek for the day was a gloomy one. News had reached Sergio of an overnight fire in the forest. That was where they were going today. The mood was bleak and grim. It seemed gloomy to know they were walking in search of a disaster area. It filled Katty with dread. Her heartbeat clopped heavily and a bit faster. They arrived at a large opening in the forest where yesterday it was filled with trees. Now it was a view of charred trees and perished animal skeletons.

Noxic, one of the many dirty pollutants, aimlessly hovers and drifts in the smoky air twirling in and around the burning, crackling, sap spitting trees. He can't stop the cogwheels in his head whirring and spinning. Clickety-clunk! Clickety-clunk! His slanted grin and raised eyebrows reflect his unease and concern at what is going to happen next. Where is he going to land? He was forever the optimist – it would be okay, he enthused through gritted teeth. He's an invisible polluted stinking dot, he knows. There are people moving around on the ground, at least he thinks they are people. He thinks they are the farmers setting fire to the trees and this turns into an inferno quickly ravaging the forest with intensely heated yellow and orange licking flames. There are animals running and scrambling for their lives. Noxic coughs and splutters in the billowing smoke clouds. He gulps and gasps as the dirty air gets thicker and blacker. This was never good, he fretted. He hums and hums to try and lighten the swell of mood in his dreary, heavy hearted thoughts.

'Where is everyone else?' he murmurs. He can see Polloo waving her arms around like a spinning windmill. He didn't know which way to look. His body drifts in the warm swirling current of the smoking clouds. He looks down and his stomach churns; he looks up and his head buzzes. Noxic and Polloo find themselves weaving in and out of the burning trees as they and all the other pollutants are scattered all around for miles and miles. They swish and swash in and out of the inferno's licking, orangey-red flames of scorching blistering heat. He grabs a tight hold of Polloo's hand and squeezes his eyes tight shut to block out the unfolding drama around him. He realises that both he and Polloo are now added to the pollutants and the deforestation of the rainforest. He opens his eyes and can see the sad puppy eyes of Polloo staring back at him. They are clumped along with the mass of pollutants. Splat! Splat! Splat! The pollutants are splattered amongst the burning, decaying trees. He gulps at the size of it all. Polloo's eyes glisten at the 'hell' of it all. She and Noxic and the throng of other pollutants create a blanket of black, charred soot covering every inch of tree bark and the ashen ground.

There are hundreds of thousands of other pollutants swarming around them and splattering their sootiness on every sizzling branch, tree bark, leaf and the whole of the undergrowth. Embers swirl around in all directions re-igniting everything in its path. Everything burns fiercely. Everything burns to a cinder. The carpet of ashen ground grows and grows. Life shrivels and dies everywhere.

'The problem is,' Noxic frets gruffly, 'there are less trees.'

Polloo grimaces her clenched jaw. 'Less trees means less photosynthesis,' she snarls. 'That's a double whammy. That's a proper disaster.'

Less photosynthesis meant less carbon dioxide would be absorbed into the trees and more carbon dioxide is then released into the atmosphere. She was right – a proper double whammy. Noxic shook his head in disbelief, and guilt, at what he was a part of. Crikey, his thoughts bellowed. The Earth is getting even warmer. He bit his lower quivering lip. He could feel his eyes welling up.

'Oh, what an inferno disaster this is,' Noxic fumes as puffs of soot splutter out of his mouth.

Sergio's bloodshot eyes well up in fury and pain. He winces in rage at the mindless, selfish destruction of trees and animals. More trees destroyed and more animals killed. The shear devastation of the rainforest was filled with smoke tendrils and the skeletal remains of the monkeys, sloths and armadillos are scattered amongst the ashes. Jake's heart twangs. He can see Sergio is upset. Jake's eyes roam over the dying embers of the burned down trees. He squints hard around the charred tree stumps in amongst the grey-white ashen ground for any flicker of movement of life. His sonar ears ping and sweep the area, ready to zoom in on to the slightest hint of any crackle, twang, crunch, shuffle or cry for help. Wisps of smouldering smoke twirl like tentacles reaching up and taking their last puff of ashen breath. The burned down trees leave an ash strewn floor, and the heat was still pulsing radiant heat underfoot.

It is like a crematorium for trees – eerie, silent and desolate. The charcoal smell grapples and clings to the back of his throat. Jake's speckling eyes tingle. Much to Jake's irritation, he was breathing in the carbon dioxide pollutants. It was the same familiar tangy acidic taste that he remembers when he was visiting Nan and Gramps in the city, smog and stinking car exhausts billowing out smoke and fumes. It was spookily all too familiar and disgusting. If it was all too familiar, he conceded, then it could only mean that the pollutants were everywhere. From Brumfield Primary school in Redditch to the Amazon rainforest in Brazil. He was gobsmacked. *Yuk!* It suddenly dawned on him the magnitude of a world filled with pollutants.

Jake pictures the pollutants whooping, hollering and hooting with joy as they freely scatter and splatter soot on everything in sight, and that included him too. He felt smeared and blackened from head to toe like it was seeping through his skin and drifting into his lungs. He had to breathe, right? There was so much of the stuff, he fumed. The destruction sickened him. It was part of everything he touched, everything he smelled and everything he tasted. The pollutants couldn't be avoided. He had to breathe it in. No matter how much he covered his mouth with his hands or wrapped a scarf or bandana around his face, the stinking soot and grime clung to his throat. It made him gag. *Urgh! Yuk!* Sergio's voice broke into his thoughts.

'We have found a lot of animal skeletons amongst the ashes,' said Sergio, shaking his bowed head. 'It is impossible for them. Even the fast and agile monkeys can't escape the raging flames of the fires at times. The animals try to outrun the raging fire, but they are chased down by the ferocious rapid licking flames.' Sergio didn't have to spell it out. His pale sad face said it all.

Singed, frazzled fur. Burned skin. Killed. Charred skeletons.

'What you see is the devastation and there are so many animals that die, and their bones are buried in the ashes.' Sergio wipes away the tears trickling down his cheeks and he gently pats his stinging eyes with a handkerchief. Some animals do manage to survive but many have badly burned bodies and limbs and scorched fur. They might just be lucky enough to be rescued and cared for by one of the animal rescue centres.

Sergio warns Katty and Jake about the ugliness of the images on his phone from the rescue centres of the burned and bandaged animals. The pictures on his phone were of a selection of animals that Katty hadn't even seen in the forest. There was a picture of a giant anteater with badly burned legs lying down on its side, drinking from a plate; a toucan stood still pitifully on the ground with fractures to its wings; one image of an exhausted, dehydrated armadillo leaning against a steel mesh wall with droopy sad eyes, and a sloth half-clinging onto the base of a tree with all of its fur frazzled away and blotchy, red burned skin. Its eyes glistened in pain as it looked pleadingly into the camera lens. Katty felt its pain and distress. It looked bewildered, confused and lost. She and Jake peer, open mouthed, into Sergio's phone screen. The images gave only a little glimpse of the plight of these defenceless creatures. It was heartless and cruel, she seethed. Not all the images told the full story because not all the animals survived their plight to survive. Sergio's screen blinks to black and he slips the phone back into his jacket pocket.

Katty takes a deep, despairing intake of breath and exhales dozily to compose her emotions. She blinks, lifts her head, and squints up the dangly high-reaching length of the nearby surviving trees. She pauses for thought and tries to contemplate what it must be like for the birds and monkeys, way high up in the forest canopy. The birds and monkeys would be fretting in despair as they watch their world being chopped down and burned to ashes all around them. Thoughts swirl around Katty's mind as she looks and scours the underside of the tree canopy. She huffs out her frustration and desperately sympathises with the animals' constant threat of pain and death. Katty blinks her thoughts into fast forward. Her thoughts pause. She can't help but grimace. Sergio's phone images of a distressed sloth, toucan and giant anteater were all real. She tries to compute the day by day destruction of the Amazon rainforest as it increases and gets worse. Every square metre by square metre is just erased of trees to the size of three football fields every minute. Every minute of every day. These thoughts scream, yell and echo a ringing shrill in her head.

Astonishing… *boom!*

Mindboggling… *boom!*

All this is disappearing every single day into a flat nothing. A flat nothing is what is left for the animals where their world is shrinking, their families are dying and their offspring are being orphaned. Their world is disappearing; their existence declining and dwindling away; the Earth's lungs shrinking, choking and wheezing. It is like gasping for an oxygen mask, praying for an inhaler and a second chance.

Smouldering ground; smouldering tears.

She had noticed the sticky, trickling sap that bleeds and weeps from the stump of a chopped tree. It had been burned to charcoal ash and the odour coming off the sap pinged her nostrils like a sickly butterscotch toastie. It's almost as if Katty can imagine and feel the pain of the tree as it is being cut down. Her stomach flip-flops. Her mind flickers in squinted eyes as the trees lose their energy, their sap, their life. She shudders. It could so easily be Lofty or Spike. Even the Mystrees could not walk or run quick enough to escape.

The tree sap oozes out of the gaping exposed trunk, extinguished by the fire and ash and now drained of substance and life. This is the tree's life left to the fate of human destruction. This was unbelievable to Katty, yet it was actually happening in front of her eyes. She was witness to this, and she was determined to get a campaign up and running when she got back to Brumfield Primary School. Miss Violet would help her. She was sure of that.

Just let anyone try stopping me after seeing this, Katty seethes with a steely-eyed determined stare. *Phew!* She huffs out an exhale of breath.

* * * * * *

Other pollutants fill the air and tarnish the trees and ground. Deeco could just make out Germie levitating in a mass crowd of other dirty, stinking pollutants. They all sway and swirl in unison on the billowing smoke-filled air currents. Deeco grunts and growls, grinding his teeth in annoyance. Everything irritates him and everyone annoys him. They were all useless, cowardly, and idiots, he protests to himself. His permanent scowling frown reflects his frustration at life, whether he is clean oxygen or polluted carbon dioxide. He can't help being a grumbling grouch and he feels he has every reason to be grumpy, especially as he has been turned into a dirty stinking pollutant. It hadn't been his choice. He didn't start the fire to deliberately burn down the trees to make way for farming land.

'Yippee! Woohoo! Get in there!,' whoops Deeco. 'Black, grey, black, grey – soot and ash. Yes! Pollute, pollute,' he yells. 'It's all their own fault.' He wasn't the one who burns down the trees.

'So there,' he grunts in protest, jutting out his jaw and pointing his index finger in the direction of Germie and to anyone else who would care to take notice. He didn't care if he irritated any of them by his actions or what he thought of them. He knew what they thought of him. The other pollutants think he is a miserable nasty grumpy fool!

'Yikes,' bleats Deeco. 'Oh no, oh no, oh no.' A sudden gust of black swirling pollutant-infested smoke whooshes through the orangey-red licking flames and heat-scorched wilting trees. He is whipped up in a loop-the-loop somersault and it catapults him directly and forcefully into a crumbly charred branch of a tree.

CRRRRUNCH!

Stars fill his dizzy head. He gasps for breath. His body is contorted, awkwardly twisted, and he is firmly wedged inside the crinkly cracks of the charred crispy bark. He can't help but splutter a gagging cough as his chest wheezes for any smidgen of oxygen there might be amongst the choking cloud of ashen soot. His head is thumping and pounding to the beat of his crestfallen and battered heart. He grunts and growls yet again and scowls at anyone who might be watching him.

'Idiots!' he spat out. 'Idiots! All of them are idiots.' He huffs. At least the wheezing coughs had stopped, much to his relief and, of course, much to his annoyance too.

'Urgh! Chaos… everywhere,' he groans at his uncomfortable jam. His eyes blink and flicker like an automatic camera shutter taking in every image at the scene in front of him.

He can see the chaos and mayhem all around him. He can see the masses of other pollutants too in chaos as they collide into each other in small puffs of soot. The rampaging, plundering pollutants crash, crunch and thud into the surrounding trees and branches. Deeco flexes, tenses, and strains his muscles against the charred bark.

'Grrrrr,' he grumbles. He is fuming with rage. His face reddens. He was now well and truly wedged into the bark of a branch. He was a crumbly, smudgy, black soot pollutant.

'Urgh! Typical,' he spat out, seething at his bad luck. He was completely stuck inside the charred bark. Tears of rage begin to well up in his reddening, stinging, bleary, bloodshot eyes. He could feel a slight give and flexing bend in the bark as he wriggled his body vigorously in frantic panic. It didn't take much for his simmering anger to explode into an ear piercing rant.

'Come on! You stupid branch. Budge a little!' he growls loudly. He pushes with every quivering muscle of strength he could muster from his tired, constricted limbs. His eyes burn and sting. More tears trickle and sizzle down his cheeks. His body shudders as his volcanic bloodstream began to spew out lava through his veins. His black soot pollutant form wriggles, kicks, *flexes, wriggles some more until a slight bendy creak gives way. Finally, and gasping breathlessly, he finds himself unstuck and no longer embedded in the bark.*

'Phew,' he pants. He half-sat up rockily, shoulders slumped, puffing out tired breaths of sooty air. His black smeary body was perched on the tree's scorched, crackling branch. Deeco sighs and wonders if he will be stuck where he is or if he'll move again when the flames return, or when a gust of wind dislodges him. He just didn't know. He really didn't care at that moment either. What he did know was that in his transformed state as a pollutant it didn't bode well for the trees, the ground, the animals or the people.

CRUNCH!

Deeco lifts his weary head. Out of nowhere Germie had crash-landed a few metres in front of him. A puff of soot quickly dispersed, and he could see Germie's legs wiggling in the air. Another 'crunch', another pollutant crashes into the branch. He was getting another headache as more and more pollutants thudded with a crunch into the burned branches and tree trunk.

'Nope,' he growls in a snarling, disgruntled huff. 'I am toxic. They are toxic too.' He has no choice but to stay put and await his fate. It was never going to be a good fate, he supposed. Whether he moved or didn't... pollution is pollution, and that spelled bad news.

* * * * * *

As Katty, Jake, Mum and Dad trudge carefully along the edge of the vast burnt out smouldering clearing, Sergio explains that the echoey screeches and howls belong to lost animals. Some were parents calling out for their offspring, others were of offspring desperately pleading for their parents to find them. Anteaters, sloths, monkeys and parrots had all become orphans, if they had not already perished in the inferno fires and toxic smoke. The cries bawled, sobbed and shrieked all day and into the night. The animals think, in hope, they are separated and trying to find each other. Sergio thinks the animals' parents have perished in the fire. The shrilling, gurgling screams for help from the orphans are chilling, desperate, wailing cries of despair – not knowing if they can survive without their parents. Alone and afraid; alone and vulnerable. Katty imagines a stressed out monkey with bulging, staring bloodshot eyes. She can hear the pain in its pleading voice, begging for anything to stop the burning trees. The monkeys desperately cling on for dear life onto the hanging tree branches. Katty frets. This is the monkey's home. The tears spill dry from the monkey's pleading eyes. A hopeless plea for help. Katty shudders. The monkey's pain rings out gloomily in her mind, she can hear the eerie shrill of the monkey's trilling, quivering tonsils.

The screeching birds, screaming monkeys and squealing sloths plead for help. They might not survive for tomorrow, seethes Katty. Her eyes tingle at the thought, at the lyrics and at the despair of another baron patch of forest land burned down and destroyed. However hard Katty tried, the smouldering stench still tingled her nose. There was still the tangy, gagging taste from the fragmented residue of the plumes of smoke prickling at the back of her throat. She felt as though she was a part of history. A bleak history. It was an ever-increasing fear of the world sleepwalking into a natural disaster.

'A disaster so bad and destructive means we need to do things today. Today, to give a chance of survival for tomorrow and the day after.' These were Sergio's tearful spluttering, pleading words after surveying another vast area of charred, treeless, flattened patches of scorched land. Jake complained he could still smell the smoke up in his nostrils.

* * * * * *

A film of wetness glazed Katty's eyes as she scanned the desolate charred ground all around her feet. She felt a shiver shoot down her back. Goosebumps prickled her skin. Her feet were stuck to the ground and all she could do was stare at Mum, Dad and Jake as Sergio crouched down and crept forward, his hand raised for everyone to stop. Jake frowns. But Sergio wasn't stopping, he thought. They gingerly tiptoe on the crispy, clumpy chunks of black charcoal and the dusty grey ashen ground.

Sergio lightly scrapes a stick through the debris as he scours the clumpy, crumbling, dusty ashen carpet. It seemed a little odd to Jake. Had Sergio lost something? Mum and Dad frowned at Katty, not sure of what was happening. What could have Sergio lost and when? Jake walked crunchingly towards Sergio to help him with whatever it was he was looking for. As he approached to within a few feet, Sergio stopped, paused and tentatively stoops down, gently prodding his fingers into the loose black and grey debris. Jake stopped too.

Sergio removes his navy blue bandana, and he reaches down to the ground. He shuffles his hands to fold and wrap the bandana. His hands slowly lift a bundle in the bandana. The bundle is a little baby mammal.

Jake couldn't make out what it was with its singed fur. He thought it might be a little monkey. Squeals and shrieks bleat out from inside the bundled bandana. Sergio places the bundle, wrapped snug in the bandana into a zip pocket of his rucksack. The snout of what Jake now realised was a baby sloth pokes out from beyond the zip. Sergio placed the rucksack back on but to the front of him so he could see the back of the baby sloth's head. The sloth's fur was scorched, singed and frizzled; raw red blemishes of burned skin were exposed. It would need to see a vet, Jake supposed. It might have been the one sole survivor left in the ruins of the trees who hadn't actually managed to escape the smouldering ruins of the fire-stricken inferno. Katty's glazed, wet eyes watch the baby sloth. She thinks of its mum and dad. What if there was no mum and dad anymore? How many had perished… and for what? Greed.

Small wisps of curling smoke rise from the eerie, smouldering, grey-ashen tree stumps. *Déjà vu* came to Katty's mind. She couldn't help but know for sure that there were more skeletal remains of animals on the ground. She knew that it was not possible for all the monkeys, sloths and other animals to have escaped the fierce, raging fireball. The perished animals had not been quick enough. It made Katty's stomach lurch upwards, and she wanted to puke. Her eyes stung and bled out tears. She gagged, coughed and dropped down to her knees. Her shoulders rocked with her head bowed down, dripping floods of tears. A constant drone of buzz filled her head as the whirring hum of hopelessness took over her quaking body. Dad gently put his hand on her shoulder, cupped his other hand under her arm and gently lifted her limp body back to her feet. He held her tight and whispered *shushes* into the side of her head. Katty sobbed, shuddered and quaked. Mum reached across to stroke her head.

'It's okay to cry, Katty. It's okay. Just let it all out,' murmurs Mum, cupping her hands around Katty's face and kissing her forehead before wrapping her arms around her in a squeezy embrace. Katty did want to let it all out like Mum had said. She wanted to let it all out in raging screams and bellowing shouts. She wanted to kick, punch, scream and yell over and over again without stopping until somebody heard her and did something about it. Her heart aches and bounces off her ribcage as her chest squeezes down on her gasping sobs. It was so cruel. It was barbaric, heartless and senseless.

Murderous, she seethes with bloodshot stinging eyes.

CHAPTER 9

Miss Ambassador

The walk back to camp had been heavy and bleary-eyed for Katty. The time passed by through the chirping, squawking treetops and screeching monkeys. It was all too familiar now to distract Katty from any miserable thoughts, but she was glad to back at the camp to distant her emotions from the ruthless reality of destruction and cruelty she had witnessed.

Katty sighed in relief as she lumbered her heavy feet into the campsite area with the familiar tranquil, calm cabins dotted around her.

Sudden crunchy steps trudge towards them. Who or what could it be? A stranger turning up out of nowhere – well, a stranger stomping with a heavy rucksack and wearing a black and green bandana and matching face mask. The stranger trundled in big, strapped-up hiking boots through the tall clumps of grass, with a distinct sound of humming.

Humming? Who would be humming in the middle of a rainforest? No. No, it couldn't be. Could it? Katty looks to Jake, and he looks to Katty. It was more than a hum, it was singing. Yes, definitely words in a tune. It did sound familiar. Katty and Jake strained their ears to catch the lyrics.

Dum, dum, dum, da, da, da... you shoot me down, but I won't fall. I am titanium, chirps the strange voice.

'I know that voice... and the tune. It can't be the singer, Sia, can it?' mutters Katty to herself. Jake frowns and tilts his head with squinted eyes.

'Really, Katty?' Jake huffs in disbelief. 'Is that what's really going on in your head? Sia, out here in the middle of the Amazon rainforest. Oh, she must be on tour!' he exclaims sarcastically.

'Yeah, but–'

Jake interrupts impatiently. 'I don't reckon it is Sia, Katty. But... but then who I'm thinking of doesn't make any sense either.'

'Nooooo way. Oh my gosh. No way,' squeals Katty, jumping up and down like a little bunny rabbit.

'Yes way,' whoops Jake. Katty smiles at Jake and they both look back in the direction of the least expected person in the most unexpected place. She knew it didn't make sense, but her head was spinning with elated joy. Jake can't believe what he is seeing. Is he hallucinating? Has he been transported back into the classroom at Brumfield Primary school? He shook his head to clear the cobwebs.

'Miss,' they both called out rushing forward, and they both flung themselves into her open arms. They all laughed and giggled.

'I suppose we'd better get on and do another campaign, shall we?' Miss Violet declared. Katty clapped and Jake nodded.

Miss had explained that since their last environmental campaign to stop car engines idling outside of schools, she had had a very special honour placed upon her.

That was why she was a little late arriving, she conceded. That sounded a bit grand, thought Katty.

A big surprise had happened. Miss Zoe Violet had been appointed as the Climate Sciences Ambassador for Schools by the Government's Department for Education. Ambassador Violet would be responsible for putting together climate issues with science and making an all-schools national campaign. And so, the 'Stop Idling' Brumfield Primary school campaign had already become a national campaign for all schools too. Surely Miss Violet would be feeling like royalty. Madam Ambassador is how she could be addressed or just simply Ambassador Violet. Or just 'Miss.' Katty would stick with 'Miss' for now. She supposed Miss was proper influential hard titanium now. The thought made Katty chuckle inside.

Katty settles her aching legs, outstretching them on the cabin porch. She was relaxed and happy to know Miss Violet was settling into her own cabin. Every time she closed her eyes Katty couldn't shake off the feeling that there were hidden, prying eyes boring into her. They could be tribes who were like ghosts drifting in and out but never seen, blending into the forest. Were these the prying, beady eyes of menacing, leering loggers, farmers, ranchers or a hungry jaguar or, worse still, the mysterious Yeti – or was it just her paranoia? Her heart pounded, pinged and clattered into her ribcage. Her mind raced and her eyes darted in all directions.

She could see blurry wobbling faces. She could hear jabbering, bumbling whispers. Her fuzzy head looks up into the blurred green canopy and she tries to talk to the Mystrees, pleading for them to help her. She can't make out their whispering words. The roots are flailing, dangling in the air and reaching out to her so Katty stretches an arm to grab onto a root but she can't quite reach. Her eyes flicker and blink. She is trying to focus through the blurs. There's Miss Violet. *Oh*, she frowns. Her eyebrows squish down then ping up. *Oh, okay.* Katty blinks hard and looks again. It's Miss. It's definitely Miss but she looks like a toucan with her white neck, yellow face and a large beautiful, bright orange and black-tipped bill. Miss is perched on a branch grunting her infamous snorting, chirping squawk.

Squawk!... 't-t-ti-ti-ta-ta-titanium' ...*squawk!*

Squawk!... 't-t-ti-ti-ta-ta-titanium' ...*squawk!*

Katty felt fuzzy. She blinks her eyes again more rapidly as she tries to reboot her brain to clear her head. Her brain was scrambled. She shook her head. Things didn't look right, everything was swirly, distorted, bewildered. She felt chilly and sweaty. Giddiness quivered from her head to her toes, and she wobbled like jelly, but somehow she managed to stay upright. Had she gone mad like Jake had so often called her? Was she infected with some kind of fever virus? She couldn't think straight. *Oh, flippity-flip*, Jake was right, she was mad! Her head whooshed and whizzed like a swirling, spinning top and her stomach was doing bouncy, flip-flopping somersaults. She needed to switch off the light and hope this was just a bad dream. *Please, please be a bad dream.* Her body was twirling; she was turning around and around, pirouetting like a befuddled ballerina, frantically looking up and down. She felt nauseous. Her face presented a clammy whiteness. *Oh, heck.* Had the Mystrees cast a dizzying spell on her? Was she even awake? *Oh, gee whiz.* She'd been well and truly zombified.

In a swooping instant she felt her body being squeezed and squished. *Urgh*, she exhaled. She felt all floppy and empty of energy. There was more grappling and squeezing. It was Mum. Mum had grabbed Katty's spinning, twirling body and her flailing arms and she was now holding Katty in a tight, squeezy hug. Katty didn't care that she was suffocating. The spinning top in Katty's head spun slower and slower and the whirring hum slowed down to a whining, stuttering stop as she held her breath. What breath she had left. Voices outside her head echoed, pinging in and out.

'It's okay, baby. It's okay,' Mum pants, stroking her hair, 'I've got you. I've got you. It's okay. Breathe, Katty, breathe. There's a good girl.'

Katty gasped a cough and sucked in small, rapid gasps of air. Her lungs pumped oxygen into her body and her cheeks began to colour. Her shoulders rocked, her chest heaved raspy breaths as she sobbed and sobbed into Mum's shoulder. Jake hugged onto Mum and Katty too.

* * * * * *

Katty is propped up in bed. Mum pats Katty's forehead with a cool, damp hand towel and offers Katty a bright yellow mug. It is filled to the brim with chocolate fruit juice. Mum holds the mug while Katty slurps steadily through a straw to feed her brain and body back to normal. Mum had been instructed by Sergio to give Katty plenty of liquids. Katty wasn't complaining. She was sure Jake would be, but she didn't really care. This was too good to complain about.

'Mmmm. Yum, yum,' cooed Katty. She instantly felt her body getting a boost. Mum took a sip. Then Mum took another sip, and then another sip. Katty gave her best disapproving frown followed by a groaning grunt. Mum took another sip. *Really, Mum?* Katty began to wonder if there would be any chocolate fruit juice left for her. After all, she was the one suffering. Like proper suffering. Like proper hallucinating stuff and going stir crazy and mad. Mum was supposed to be looking after her, not helping herself to all the choco–

'Wow!' interrupted Mum, with a gulp and satisfying gasp – after yet another long sip of cupuaçu. Mum's tongue crackled, popped and oozed with a wondrous sensation trickling down her throat. She gasped her delight at the taste.

'That's proper lush, Katty,' Mum oozed, 'it really is lush.'

Katty rolls her eyes in disbelief. 'Is it, Mum? I can't remember 'cos I haven't had any for a while.'

'Oh!' startles Mum, 'here darling, have some more.'

'Are you sure there is any left?'

'Oh, yes. There is plenty left, Katty. Don't mind me.' Mum reaches out the half-filled cup and offers it up to Katty's mouth. 'You have as much as you want, sweetheart.'

Mum filled Katty with plenty of reassurance after her traumatic and extremely embarrassing episode in the jungle. Katty slowly regains her senses. Sergio had suggested to Mum that the hallucinations were probably temporary, mild side-effects from a mosquito bite. The vampire blood sucking mosquitoes had struck.

'You were proper weird, Katty,' whispers Jake, 'even more than usual.'

Katty gives a meek dimpled lopsided grin. She wasn't impressed, her face reddens. She felt a little bit embarrassed. Mum had insisted Katty go straight to bed. No complaints there, decided Katty. Anything to get away from the fuss and attention. She needed space. She needed sleep. It was a matter of minutes before she entered deep into the land of nod. She snoozes behind the mosquito netting, safe from any further hallucination and wild mad-girl antics. The whirring emotions swirl around her mind, dipping up and down, and in and out of her sleepy, dreamy thoughts. Her eyelids flicker rapid blinks; her mouth and lips twitch and tighten. Her body rocks, tosses and turns, twists and jolts.

Katty bolts upright in bed from her sleep, her throat shrills out a warbling, echoey, screeching lumberjack's yell.

'TIMBER!' Katty's warbling shrill echoes and shakes the cabin's wooden bedroom.

The decibels reverberated into deafening, shuddering, trembling echoes. The loud boings shook the bamboo ceiling and walls all around her. Her head is throbbing and her ears are ringing out loud. She is frantically gasping and sucking in air. Her chest is wheezing as she props her quivering body up by her arms in bed. Her beetroot cheeks glow.

Thud, crash, bang.

Mum bursts into the bedroom, stumbling in a flustered panic with flushed cheeks and heavy panting. Katty stares wide eyed, blowing heavy through trembling lips. She sniffles, puffs out her cheeks and turns to look at Mum.

'I think I just chopped down a tree, Mum,' gasps Katty, 'I might have killed Lofty or Spike.'

Mum sat herself on the bed and put her arm around Katty's shoulder.

'Katty. No, you didn't chop down a tree. You wouldn't, you couldn't.' Mum pauses. The cogwheels twirl and smoke inside Mum's confused head. 'Who are Lofty and Spike?'

'I don't know, Mum,' blushes Katty. If Mum knew she talked to trees... well, who knows what might happen! 'I'm all confused.' Katty hoped that would explain it and the probing questions would stop.

Mum smiled. 'If anyone was to chop down a tree, it would be your Dad! And even he couldn't do that by having a bad dream.'

Katty had startled everyone in the cabin, including herself. Her breathing calmed down and she felt drained. Mum kissed her forehead and Katty strained a lopsided grin in an attempt to reassure Mum that she was okay. Katty could see the worry in Mum's wet-filmed glistening eyes. Katty's eyebrows dipped down in concern, wrinkling her forehead. It was only a bad dream, she supposed. The bedroom was empty again and yet in her mind she could see the logger's beady red eyes glow in the darkness beyond the bed's mosquito net. *Brrrr!* Shudders ripple goosebumps down her spine.

Chapter 10

Walls Of Water

Shadowy trees lean and overstretch across the river as they overhang and crouch on the riverbank edges, darkening the flat waters. There are plops and rippling splashes in the distance. Katty's eyes narrowed. She squints her eyes to focus on what looks like bobbing heads. These were definitely not friendly-looking pink dolphins. There was a more predatory, eerie, sinister tone to the plonk, plop and gurgle as the bulbous, shiny, marble green eyes glided along the river's surface. She gulped hard. Those eyes belong to menacing caiman alligators seeking out their lunch. Katty involuntarily gasps and gulps again. She clutches tightly onto her life jacket. Jake leans forward, stretches his neck like a curious giraffe. His eyes flash wide open, his mouth gapes open as he too spots the prehistoric dinosaur's bulbous eyes peering back at him. There are other bubbles splattering the surface too. Maybe there was a shoal of red bellied piranhas lurking just beneath the surface of the river just waiting to munch and devour its prey to the bone. Jake didn't like the idea of being their prey. He sat up rigid and folded his arms across his life jacket. Better safe than sorry.

* * * * * *

The hours had tumbled in and out of her dreams and before she knew it, she had done her cleansing of the teeth, brushed her knotted hair and was at the breakfast table munching on a banana slice pancake. She wanted to be energised for the day ahead. It meant an early morning start and a *very, very* long drive out of the Amazon rainforest and travel further down into the south of Brazil to reach the Foz de Iguazu. *Phewee!* Finally, they arrive. Katty jumps down, stretches her legs, arms and back with some yoga stretches. Her heart flutters at the thought of what lay ahead.

Their feet crunch along the short walk on the narrow gravelled path to the boat access platform. Katty, Jake, Mum, Dad and Sergio don their life jackets and step into the rigid-hulled inflatable boat. It was a proper sporty speedboat version of their green hulled wooden riverboat. They sit in the front row of seats. The front row proved to be a guarantee for getting maximum waterfall rain spray, reflected Katty. She was sopping wet right through to her skin and bedraggled, just like a drowned rat.

Jake gasps at the Iguazu Falls. His jaw lolled, his eyes twinkle and he blinks for a few moments in awe. He was hypnotised, Katty guessed. Only Mum's laser stare could normally hypnotise him! Jake was so excited he began to do little bunny hops, clapping his hands and a beaming wide smile covered his face. Mum and Dad leant into each other with Dad putting his arm around Mum's shoulder. Katty grinned in awe too, as Sergio pointed to the tops of the mass of waterfalls before their very squinty eyes.

'Oh, wow! Katty, look. It's awesome. I bet Miss Violet wishes she was here,' Jake continues to clap excitedly like an applauding seal. Katty nodded in agreement and grins in wonderment. It's not often she agreed with Jake, but seriously… wow! It seems to literally suck the air out of her lungs and take her breath away. She grins again.

'Yes, Jake, you're right. It really is awesome.'

It was a pity Miss had decided to miss the trip to stay in camp to collect pollutant samples but it was important so she could produce scientific findings with her samples and experiments as part of her Ambassadorial role in Climate Sciences for schools. Katty rubs her hands because that would include *their* campaign too, she enthused with glee and excited anticipation. She couldn't wait to get involved in the next campaign, especially after the success of the 'Stop Idling' car engine campaign outside the school. She grinned; her chest lifted with pride. That campaign had definitely made a difference and there was far less parking and engine idling, and far more parents and children walking, and far cleaner air because of it.

Sergio continues to point at the spectacular walls of magnificent waterfalls cascading down in front of them. He was giving them a running commentary.

'The height of the waterfalls ranges from between sixty metres and eighty-two metres. It is fact,' he nodded. 'The Iguazu Falls is nearly three times as wide and twice as high as Niagara Falls.'

'It's amazing,' enthused Katty. Her eyes sparkle. 'And just look at all the rainbows everywhere. Wow!' She half grins at the strange yet magnificent sight of hundreds of swooping, scattered, bendy, curving, arching rainbows right before her bewildered eyes.

They were witnessing the Iguazu Falls, one of the natural wonders of the world. Katty peers along its endless curtains of 275 waterfalls spanning across over two and a half kilometres wide in front of her starry eyes. Wherever they looked there were waterfalls. On one side of the Iguazu Falls is Argentina and on the other side is Brazil.

They were slap bang in the middle between Argentina and Brazil. Katty peeks up to the top edge of the waterfalls – all the way up as high as eighty-two metres. That's like the height of New York's Statue of Liberty or it's like a bit higher than the Taj Mahal in India's city of Agra, she gushed. Sergio had handed out cagoules for each of them. Jake stretched out an arm to give Sergio a fist-bump as 'thanks'. Sergio gladly obliged his fist-bump back with a water soaked beaming smile. Katty clenched her fist and squinted a mischievous frown. She wanted to stretch out a swinging arm to offer Jake a fist-bump to his arm! Only joking, she mused. She couldn't resist the thought as she tried to muffle the chuckles to herself. Instead, she decided to punch the air. Wasted, she thought, no arm of Jake available for her to give him a friendly jab from his favourite queenie big sis. Respect, little bro!

One thing was for sure, no matter where you were in the Iguazu Falls, you were definitely going to get absolutely soaking wet. Katty thought it would be easier wearing a swimsuit. Jake would prefer to be wearing a wetsuit, flippers and goggles! There was no escaping the shear wetness in the air like being in a waterpark. They stood in awe at the shear magnificence of the Iguazu Falls. It was truly mind-blowing and magnificent and extremely wet, but it felt cool.

It's an incredible sight and proper weird at the same time, gawped Katty. She could literally see hundreds of rainbows bending and arching right across the spectacular spray of waterfalls, and more waterfalls, and yet even more waterfalls. A gigantic curtain of waterfalls was strewn to her left in Argentina and to her right in Brazil. She knew she was in the middle of the Iguazu River, and she knew if she stretched her arms out far enough to either side she could be in both Argentina and Brazil at the same time. Instead, she decided to stay sat down in the front row of the rigid-hulled inflatable speedboat as it jerked, rocked and swayed in amongst the constant burbling, swishing whoosh of the waterfall's overflowing taps as they gush over the high cliff edges and spill into the Iguazu River. The water spray was everywhere. She was drenched in the steam-like water mist.

Katty gulps in disbelief. The waterfalls were just absolutely everywhere all around her, like being stood in the bottom of a gigantic bathtub surrounded by walls of water.

'This was definitely real,' she cooed. She wouldn't have believed it otherwise. She couldn't peel the smile off her face, she was so happy. The boat pirouettes and leans to the port side as it spins around and trundles serenely back to the rickety wooden jetty. Katty blinks the wet mist away and savours the moments in open-mouthed silence.

Only after disembarking the boat and stretching her stiffened legs did Katty start to feel a bit sad as she reluctantly handed back her life jacket. Her mind still whirred at the marvels, the awesome views and even the soaking wetness of the Iguazu Falls. The adrenaline rush gently seeped out of her veins as the exhilarating euphoria waned away, but she wanted to cling on a little longer and she didn't want to let it go.

The exhausting *very* long bumpy drive back up to the Amazon rainforest through the tyre-worn ruts in the dusty road rocked them judderingly from side to side and stirred the weariness from their aching bodies.

They disembarked wearily from the rickety trucks and donned their rucksacks on for a short trek along the riverbank to their campsite for the night. Katty was knackered and running on adrenaline. It had been an exhilarating day for sure. It had been a long exhausting day, and she couldn't wait to have some food and chillax.

The terraced eco-cabins greet her glinting eyes. They all felt wearily fatigued from a fulsome day with plenty of chitter-chatter, gorging down some food, scampering around their cabins to be mosquito protected for a yawning, deep, grateful sleep. She couldn't wait for another new day with a short drive and another trek. Katty felt she was now quite a good trekker and would consider doing the Duke of Edinburgh's Bronze Awards – she'd easily do two days and one night with six hours activity each day. Her head sunk deep into the pillow and her bones slunk restfully into the mattress.

Katty must have zonked out as soon as her head hit the pillow. It just proved, she assured herself, how much hard work it was looking after a little, smarmy, annoying know-it-all brother. Not that he ever appreciated it... or her. Her eyes flicker open to the warm air of morning heat and chorus of chirping birds outside. She felt refreshed from her slumber, and she was glad to know that no vampire mozzies had managed to feast on her blood – no bites to report.

She wonders if today will not involve another crisis. No crisis for Katty would mean no fires, no orphaned sloths, and no charging attack from a Yeti. Less of a crisis, but still disgusting is Jake farting and Mum and Dad kissing.

Yuk! Urgh!

She grins in hope. *Phew!* She sighs in relief. *Oh, heck!* She clasps her hands together as she looks forward to the day.

* * * * * *

The morning trek involves Katty, Jake, Mum, Dad, Sergio and Miss Violet beavering in amongst the trees and scurrying inside the undergrowth. They carefully collect healthy samples of the forest plants, twigs, leaves and bits of tree bark for Miss Violet. The samples are delicately placed inside small plastic bags and into each other's rucksacks. Miss Violet would use the samples for science classes in Brumfield school. The return trek to the campsite, so Miss Violet had decided, meant they would follow close to the riverbank. The river glistens, the sunrays bounce brightly off the water, dazzling Katty's eyes. She blinks a hard squint. Her eyesight is blurred for a few seconds but her vision gently returns into focus. She can see clearly again.

U-u-urgh! her throat stammers. *Gulp!*

Katty's body freezes stiff. *Horror!* Her bulging wide-eyed stare is firmly fixed on the sight of a ginormous 'alligator' black caiman. The alligator is staring straight back at her. A moment ago, she was hot and sweaty, and now her skin turns into a cold, prickly chill.

Oh, flippity-flip!

Tingling sparks of anxiety sweep through her body like a tsunami of scary tremors rushing up from her wriggling toes into her buzzing brain.

Brain freeze! Her brain scrambles and flickers but she stays frozen.

Heeeeelp! She urges her brain to do something. *Ctrl-Alt-Delete.*

Brain... quick... unfreeze!

Reboot – Refresh! She appeals again.

Katty thought, what could go wrong? *Gulp!* The black caiman might charge and clamp its jaw onto her and fling her somersaulting into the river for another black caiman in waiting. *Munch! Munch!*

Oh, gruesome! she shudders. Maybe Dad would dive onto the black caiman's scaley back and wrestle with it, clinging onto its thick muscley neck and rolling around in the sticky slippery, slimy mudbank. *Oh,* Katty contemplates. *Ouch!* Dad would probably faint first!

Mum grasps a firm grip on Jake's upper sleeves. Mum imagines Mum would grapple him like a rag doll and scarper, full pelt, deep into the jungle, zigzagging and screaming. *She,* Katty, would unfreeze her frightened frozen body, spin on her toes 180 degrees and do the zigzag running thing too and avoid bumping into the trees. The thoughts made her feel a bit queasy and sick. Her head got giddy and light.

Jake looks up and frowns at Mum's rough grip of his sleeve. Mum's eyes are transfixed ahead of her. He follows the direction of her stare. He quaffs in a large gulpy breath, and his eyes spring out of their sockets.

'W-w-what is that?' he wheezes, pointing a quivering finger towards the riverbank. Sergio looks around clumsily to see a black caiman on the nearside bank of the river. *Their* nearside of the river. *Gulp!* winces Sergio. There is no river in between them and the black caiman, but only about twenty metres of dry land.

Usain Bolt could sprint one hundred metres in 9.58 seconds. Fact. An adult black caiman was not so fast, and it would get tired after about twenty metres. But Sergio didn't want to test that theory out... just in case it wasn't accurate.

'Okay, okay. There's a good crocodile,' gasps Sergio. The black caiman looks to be about five metres in length, snout to tail end. That's the height of a house. It probably weighs about half a tonne. That's the weight of a single decker bus. Fact. It is the largest predator and is known as a man-eater. Jake thought it was a dinosaur!

'No problem, Jake,' pipes up Sergio in a trembling whimper, 'it is only sunbathing, but don't go and join it.'

'Maybe you could go and brush its teeth,' quips Katty nervously with a wry smile. Jake rolls his eyes and tuts.

'Yeah, right. Maybe you could comb it's scaley back.'

The black caiman slowly lifts its body from the ground, haunching itself up on its legs as if it was getting ready to sprint out of the blocks... Usain Bolt style.

Jake's mouth opened, but no sounds came out. His brain shrills *man-eating alligator*. He froze. He only realises his mouth was gaping wide open when Dad lightly lifts his jaw shut and mouths 'it's okay'. Dad presses his finger to his own lips.

Shhh.

Jake's trembling lips tighten as he holds his breath. Mum stands behind him and wraps her arms around his shoulders and chest. She squeezes a firm grip to safeguard her son. Katty stands stuck in her tracks a metre behind Mum and Jake. *What about me then, Mum?* Katty frowns her annoyance. She could be eaten too, she frets. The black caiman was staring, draping open its mouthful of razor sharp teeth at her too.

She folds her arms crossly, vexed. She decides not to stare back at the menacing dinosaur beast. It occurs to Katty that no matter how fast the snapper beast was, she was the furthest away and had heard that you should run in zigzags as alligators weren't so quick at changing directions and so were rubbish at doing zigzagging themselves. The black caiman looks to be on its haunches up high and hunched upright and ready to launch out of the sprinting blocks. It was rocking slightly forward and back. She imagines that the black caiman was deciding its choice of food on the menu.

'Not today, buddy,' she whispers through chattering teeth.

Sergio reaches into his rucksack and slowly lifts out a klaxon air horn. Sergio knew a long blast of the air horn would scare off the black caiman. The black caiman's red eyes luminate fear. Those same eyes are just beyond the reach of its snout and mass array of teeth.

Mum's hug tightens. Jake can feel the tension and quivering fear in Mum's squeeze as it vibrates through him. He was suffocating, but he wasn't going to complain. She slowly releases her wrapped arms and was now tightly gripping onto his upper sleeves with clenched fists ready to catapult him out of harm's way. Jake's thought of being in harm's way didn't really reflect the dire seriousness of their situation. The harm would be very painful and deathly, he believed. The black caiman's looming presence only confirms its very real mass of menacing razor sharp teeth and the ability to clamp onto its victim. *Gulp!* Hopefully the victim is not Jake any second now. Its mouth would snap shut and hold its prey in a savage vice-like crunching jaw. Mum is prepared to fling him indiscriminately like a piece of rubbish out of harm's way. That seems a bit harsh, he thought. After all, he was only ten years old. The tension eases as Sergio takes very slow tentative steps backwards towards the others. Jake thought that Sergio was like Doctor Doolittle and that he could talk to the animals through his mind. Katty was not so convinced. What was wrong with people like Mum and Sergio? Telepathic or just tele-*pathetic*, she quips inwardly.

Sergio presses a finger to his lips for silence and with his other hand he gestures an open, hovering raised palm to indicate to the others to be quiet. Everything was in slow motion as they slowly creep away. Nobody blinks. Their eyes firmly fix on the bulbous red 'devils' eyes of their stalker. It seems to take an age for them to collectively be a safe distance from the clearing, from the riverbank, and from the prehistoric black caiman dinosaur that was raised on its four legs, smiling menacingly.

* * * * * *

Katty's scare with the black caiman had rattled and shredded her nerves. She felt her nerves had fused back together and her chattering teeth had come to a grinding stop. Her thumping heartbeat had calmed down. Her trembling body was glad to be back in the campsite. She had been in a stand-off, glaring eye to eye with a fierce, jaw-snapping black caiman. Her gibbering words splutter her shock.

'Get a grip, Katty, you're doing my head in whinging about the black caiman,' snaps Jake, scowling with gritted teeth at Katty. 'I was the closest to it, not you.'

'You mean you weren't close enough, you little–'
Ahem, ahem.

Mum's feigned cough drew both Katty and Jake's attention.

'That'll do, young lady,' growls Mum, 'you should know better than to talk to your little brother like that.'

An awkward silence held its breath. Katty bowed her head.

'Sorry, Mum,' she said.

'What about *sorry* to me?' quips Jake. 'Mum, tell her.' His eyebrows were expectantly raised. No way is that going to happen, Katty fumes, hoping Mum would not make her say *sorry* to the little worm. And she didn't. Mum turns and makes her way into the dining area. Katty catches Jake's eye and pokes out her tongue quickly. Jake blanks her; he knew it was useless now Mum had left the porch, and she was no longer listening or interested in their little squabble. Katty and Jake trundle in Mum's wake.

Jake plonks himself down and slides along the dining table's bench, planting his elbows onto the table to prop up his tired, weary, miserable head. He looked like a grumpy version of his Gramps. He hadn't realised how hungry he was. Sergio had warned him and Katty against eating anything off the forest floor as monkey droppings can be easily mistaken for chocolate peanut butter banana bites. *Oh, yuk!* gagged Jake.

Katty had thought that even Jake *'the greedy pig'* would notice the difference!

Jake's rumbling, churning stomach craves for something greasy, luscious, sweet and crispy. His head spins at the thought of a cheeseburger sloshed in sweet chilli sauce surrounded by a thick stack of salted crispy fries and washed down with an extra-large strawberry milkshake.

Aah! Yummy!

A tinge of guilt twangs his heart, pinging and resonating in his chest at the shame of wanting meat. But it would be less meat he would be eating rather than more like Sergio had suggested, and he would definitely cut down on meaty burgers. He promised that to himself. Dribbles of saliva trickle along his lower lip. Was he really dribbling or was it some sort of mirage? How cool was that? He chuckled to himself under his breath. Katty would call him a greedy little pig. But he didn't care. It wasn't the meat that was the problem, it was the destroying of the trees to clear the land to feed the cattle.

'Sergio, after the ranchers ranch their herd of beef cattle, can't they just grow the trees back then?' asks Jake. He looks quizzically towards Sergio for some hint of reassurance. He soon realises Sergio wasn't forthcoming in offering any hope with his left eyebrow elevated up near his wavy hairline.

'Duh!' exclaims Katty as she shakes her head in the direction of *dippy* Jake. She tuts and wonders how Jake's mind can be so scatterbrain and that his brain does not compute with his big fat blabbering mouth. *Does he seriously think the trees will just grow back again from the scorched, ashen ground as a quick fix? The trees reach right up high reaching up to the white fluffy clouds. Yet, Jake the dimwit does not dwell on how many years it takes for a tree to stretch that high. Seriously!* She felt embarrassed for him, and she felt ashamed to be his sister. What were Mum and Dad thinking about by having a boy? She shakes her head and tuts again in disgust. Wasn't she good enough as an only child? Was she not such an adorable daughter without adding to the family tree? Surely, Mum and Dad had regretted it since, she mused with a tinge of guilt at Mum and Dad's regret!

Jake looks at his feet and stares blankly. He sighs and he wonders what's going on under his feet. The heat and the lack of nutrients to feed the ground is turning it to dust – no hope of growth and the animals are dying. The scorched land would be farmed for a few months and then the land would be wrecked, become useless and baron with no prospect of a future. Then the farmers just simply move on to another area and the same thing happens again… and again. It becomes just dust with no chance of anything growing back on the sandy soil.

The vast open spaces of deforested land were on Jake's mind a lot, like a fly buzzing around in his head. He couldn't say it was bugging him because that's what Katty did to him. *No*, he frets, it is knowing that every minute of every day there was destruction of this awesome landscape that just takes his breath away with the really awesome animals – even the frightening black caimans took his breath away! Not only that, but a tingly, chilly ripple shivers up his spine at the thought of the trees suffering. The thought of Spike and Lofty shuffling their roots to try and run in slow motion - screaming, their bark skin crackling, their branches breaking and snapping. The destruction was cruel. Jake had thought it might be the excitement– each day a new adventure – and the odd fright of a black caiman. He just felt constantly sodden and drenched in sweat. It felt the same thing day in, day out – never really feeling fresh for long. The humidity slapped him in the face, his back, his stomach. It was like being in a sweltering oven. He now knew what Mum's chocolate brownies felt like when sweating in the oven. Hot, sticky, sizzling, unable to breathe.

CHAPTER 11

Campaign Chit-Chat!

The trudge back to camp had made Katty's legs ache and crampy. She was glad of the table bench in the dining cabin to put her feet up. Her legs oozed relief. They gathered around the dining for a well-deserved feast. The food weighs heavy and satisfying in their bellies. The table had been cleared and the day's events unfolded with Katty, Jake and Miss chit-chatting about their next campaign. Mum, Dad and Sergio hung around in chit-chat too.

How is it that the world leaders and politicians can't see the rainforest burning? fumes Katty. Miss Violet had said the burning rainforest can be seen from outer space. Katty thought about mentioning this to Tim Peake, the British astronaut, to see if he had noticed the fires from outer space while he was floating around on the International Space Station. She didn't know when she would meet Tim Peake but sensed it would be sooner rather than later! Jake, the fake *Buzz Lightyear*, would be so jealous, she smirks.

Sergio too had been startled at the images he had seen of the rainforest on his phone from the space satellite. The pictures had been from before and after the fires.

'The pictures don't lie,' scoffs Ambassador Violet. 'But the politicians, world leaders and big corporate businesses do lie, and they too are to blame for the deforestation.'

Katty felt like she should bow her head in recognition of Miss Violet's new Climate Sciences Ambassadorial role for schools for the whole of the United Kingdom.

'It's not too late to turn things around, is it Miss?' probes Katty, looking for a crumb of comfort to the devastating satellite images from space and from their own first-hand experience of charred open spaces. Miss Violet folds her arms and huffs out loud.

'I hope it's not too late, Katty. The climate impact is not coming in a few years' time,' she huffs again, pursing her lips. 'No. It's already here. Yesterday. Today. And tomorrow. Why pretend otherwise, like the world leaders and politicians do?'

Katty recalls Miss Violet illustrating in class with pictures and video clips on a PowerPoint in class. She had publicised occasions that showed politicians speaking with pointed fingers as the perspiration on their faces revealed their lies. The truth is there, exposed, and visible for all to see. As the business corporations boast of their profits as they pollute at will, the oil leaks into the rivers and seeps into the ground and the stinking, polluted soot and gases are released into the atmosphere.

'Words are cheap,' Katty spits out. She is convinced she can see steam coming out of Miss Violet's ears.

'When a politician talks about saving the environment, they're spilling more lies,' hisses Mum, 'just like the big corporate businesses do. They all pretend to care about the planet as they carry on polluting the land, sea and air. They only care about making money.'

Teardrops falling; profits calling!

Katty chides at the image of how the crocodile tears are just to disguise the lies. It's like what Jake does when Mum gives him a row – he sniffles and lets a few fake tears trickle down his cheeks. *Pathetic!* Katty frowns as she notices Jake's quizzical head tilting to one side. He must be thinking about something really important, she guessed.

'Does Dad cry often, Mum?' quips Jake, his eyebrows raised in eager anticipation.

'Yes, Jake. Whenever he gets caught stealing one of my chocolate brownies.' Mum grins and ruffles Jake's hair. 'So best I don't catch *you* pinching my chocolate brownies either.' Dad rolled his eyes and shook his head... *who... me?!*

'I won't, Mum,' grunts Jake. 'It's always Dad that does it, Mum. Honest.' Katty shook her head and grimaces a lip curling smirk in resigned disbelief. Only Jake could say 'honest' and get away with it! The little grovelling liar!

Mum and Dad joked the expedition was like their honeymoon, but with two adorable kids! They were chilled out because of how peaceful it has been since they had arrived in Brazil. They had noticed that Katty and Jake had not been fighting, bickering, or even telling tales on each other. *Lies*, fretted Katty. Wait until Mum finds out there are fewer chocolate brownies in the bottom of the bran flakes cereal box! Then we'll see who tells lies. She scowls a sideways glance towards Jake. He's no angel either. He walked and bounced around in a stupid boy strut. He must think he has a glowing yellowy-gold halo hovering above his head like he was a golden boy.

Katty reckons if Jake were to lie down in a hospital scanner machine tube filled with powerful magnets to have an MRI (Magnetic Resonance Imaging) brain scan she was sure the scan screen would spell out 'cheat'. Jake retorts that if she had a scan it would find no brain; it would be empty! He raised his hand with his palm facing Katty to stop her talking anymore.

'Nope. I don't want to hear it again. I'm not a cheat or a bad loser.' He stamps his foot. 'No,' he barks, 'talk to the hand 'cos the face ain't listening. I don't care. So there.'

Look at him, she sneers to herself, *the little worm.* Acting like he's the angel, wearing his imaginary 'halo' above his head. But she could see right through him even if Mum couldn't.

Katty raised an eyebrow. *Oh!* Jake thought. First a raised eyebrow and now she has her arms folded and she is tapping her right foot on the wooden flooring. Was that steam coming out of her ears? He supposed she was upset about something, and he had no clue what it could be!

'Once a cheat; always a cheat,' she spat, 'Mummy's boy.'

She gave him a hard stare, but Jake just blanks her. He was a bit too full of himself when Sergio was around. Katty tutted, but she didn't see the point in saying anything else. It would only make things worse, and wind her up, of course. She would bide her time. She bit her lower lip in pensive thought. She would have to find different ways of ignoring Jake and just chill out.

He never admits to cheating on the game, Mario Kart. If he could lie about that, then what else could he lie about that she didn't know about? *Every sibling for themselves,* she could imagine him saying. The little worm, always squirming in and out of trouble. Why couldn't she be Mummy's girl? Why was he always Mummy's boy? He never does his homework on time or tidies his room, and he has square eyes through constantly looking at a gaming screen. She sighs. And *she's* always the one who gets told off when they argue. She narrowed her eyes, squinting, thinking of ways how she could get her revenge on him without Mum or Dad finding out.

'Mmmm. I wonder,' she murmurs. A sly smirk creases across her face.

CHAPTER 12

Mascara Soot

Katty sat on a creaky wicker chair on the cabin porch. Her tummy rumbled. It would soon be dinner time. Her mind whirred aimlessly in a daydream about nothing until she remembered their Climate Summit meeting was tomorrow. She blinked and squinted through her black-rimmed wraparound sunglasses at the rainforest surrounding her. Only a few more sleeps to go, she echoes with a heavy heart.

The trees lean eerily above her. The same way as they had ever since she had arrived. *Spooky!* Spike and Lofty's spindly spider-leg roots shuffle and walk as they whisper ever closer to Katty, towering above her reassuringly. It gave her a comfort knowing Spike and Lofty are always nearby. The images in her head from the past week were burned deeply into Katty's mind. She blinks her wet eyes to stave off the tingling, prickling emotion at the carnage in front of her. She sniffles; she stems the flow of salty tears. The horrific destruction of the rainforest smoulders in front of her. She can see a carpet of charred ashen grey covering the ground, and the mass of short tree stumps in a large open space where there had recently been tall, gangly, luscious green, beautiful trees. Katty knew that scattered in amongst the grey ashen carpet there would be skeletal remains of helpless animals who hadn't been able to escape in time and had perished. Agonisingly, horrifically and cruelly. The mental image kept creeping up on her and searing to the surface of her thoughts at unexpected times without warning. She blinked rapidly. The billowing plumes of smoke had smarted her eyes and gagged her throat. The crispy, grey-ashen ground had crackled beneath her feet on the barren land and speckled with animal skeletons.

Crunch, crunch.

The black soot had smeared on any nearby remaining trees, branches, plants and every animal and everything, including their own clothes and skin. It had been so gloomy and disgusting her whole body drooped and shuddered at the same time. The shock, the horror and surprise had suffocated her. She had wanted to murmur 'why?' but the word would not get passed her croaking, choked throat or her trembling lips.

The black stinking grimy soot was soddened, soaked and had smeared like streaky, crazy mascara markings on the faces of Katty, Jake, Sergio, Mum and Dad. They had all looked ridiculous. It was smudged in their hair and hands and engrained in their clothes. The despicable soot was totally everywhere and totally on everything.

* * * * * *

Even Toxie the pollutant was whinging about being stuck to the disgusting humans!

Whoosh!

Toxie and Tamin rise from the burning trees. They drift up as gases to the high atmosphere and disperse as soot on the surviving trees, the grass and ground, in the rivers and they even land on animals. Yuk! Sticking to the fur of jaguar cats and the scaley backs of black caiman. Tamin swirls, spins and sways uncontrollably all over the place. She breathes a sigh of relief to a soft landing. Ah! A soft landing on the snout of a black caiman.

'Oooooh. H-h-huh. Aaaargh!' she screams.

The flames dance, lick and scorch as Toxie and Tamin scatter as plumes of carbon dioxide smoke. The pollutants spill out in mass. They are coughed and belched out in black and grey billows, spitting both Toxie and Tamin into the air. They parade freely in the air. The mass of pollutants spews out and blanket the soot on everything in its path including the trees and plants, and carpets the ground as dark smoke clouds spew out from beyond the orangey-red flickering flames. As the smoke swirls up, the bulk of pollutants swarm like a whirling murmuration of starlings in the Italian Roman sky. The thick, dense, tingling, eye-watering plumes of throat burning pungent acrid smoke is everywhere. Toxie splutters a cough and Tamin's throat gags and croaks.

Urgh! Gag!

Toxie and Tamin are amongst the throng of pollutants inhabiting the flames. They scorch the trees to form charred smouldering wood and stinking, clingy smoke-filled soot. They are the burnt crispy wood of the trees. Their chaos devours everything as they frantically scramble, collide and bustle amongst themselves in the vast blanket of the filthy, blackened, smeary army of pollutants.

Katty recalled the school experiment. This was the same as the sticky card windows experiment test that

Miss Violet had placed around the school for catching the invisible speckled black-dotted pollutant particles escaping from the car exhaust fumes. They too had been all black and charred. Katty shakes her head in disbelief and disgust.

Toxie and Tamin form parts of the thick blanket of pollutants that blackens the sky and stains and contaminates the surrounding trees, land and rivers. It is a buildup of shrieking panic, filled with anxiety that greets the plumes of smoke like rising tornadoes. The pollutants rise, swirl and twirl through the crackling sound of the burning tree bark, crackling branches and scorched leaves. The trees, branches and leaves wilt, twist and burn in the intense flames and heat.

Toxie rises from the ashes. The naked flame had ignited the trees that had been doused in fuel by the ranchers and farmers. It was utter bedlam and chaos.

Tamin's tonsils shrill a trembling, warbling yell.

'Fire, fire, fire,' shrieks Tamin as she splutters from the charred, burning tree bark. 'I've been sootified! Get out of my way.' Blinking her smarting eyes, she blindly whacks into every branch, and she bumpily drifts and swirls groggily in the dark thick clouds of choking smoke.

'Oh, what a nightmare,' she hissed.

Toxie holds his breath. He was irritated, cramped and squeezed tightly in the throng of crowded pollutants as they fizzled in between and around the burning, sizzling trees well below the forest canopy. Toxie scowls and huffs. His cheeks puff out as he bustles and shoves the other pollutants out of his way. He knew many of the pollutants were on their way up higher and higher.

They would soon be beyond the forest canopy and into the atmosphere to invade outer space to pollute the ozone layer. The pollutants bump and push him around. His irritation simmers and crackles. He bit his lower trembling lip to stem his temper.

* * * * * *

'Of course. Yes,' whispers Katty to herself, 'the rainforest is both paradise and hell rolled into one.' Even when she whispered her thoughts out loud, it still didn't make sense. The paradise is how Katty had imagined it to be. Going into the rainforest is so awesome; she can feel her lungs fill up with refreshing heartening breaths. She felt like she was opening a wardrobe door into the world of Narnia. *Awesome!* She smiles her delight; she couldn't wish to have ever been in such a beautiful forest.

Every twang of a rustling branch Katty heard merged into wispy mumblings from the mischievous Mystrees. Spike and Lofty creak, groan and shuffle their spider leg roots as they jostle to dawdle slowly around to guard the vast rainforest. *Their* jungle. A world in which Katty beams at the natural wonderland. The bright gleaming rich colours of greens, yellows and luscious reds splatter all around and serenely blend into the echoey sounds of humming, thrumming, buzzing, squawks, chirps and croaks. She has seen the astonishing Iguazu Falls with its endless curtains of magnificent, breathtaking waterfalls, miles wide and as high as the Big Ben parliamentary clock in London. She'd seen a world blessed with the native tribes that worship animal spirits and live off the land. Her head buzzes with blissful dreaminess. This was definitely paradise. All she needed was a big fluffy pillow and she could float dreamily and blissfully in her thoughts.

And then she had realised that there had been a 'hell' unleashed on the rainforest with the destruction and pollution. She had seen parts of this paradise burned, scorched and bare; treeless, empty openness and far-stretching deforested patches of land the size of towns and cities. She strains a tight grin to stave off the images of what she had witnessed firsthand. Right in front of her very eyes. She had seen for herself the large, deforested areas. Sergio had reminded her that there are yet more and more trees being cut down, burned, scorched and stripped away every day, every week, every month, every year. Katty gulps. She imagines a trap door opening and, with the conveyor belt of destruction, being swallowed up and everything falling down into a pit of hell. It felt like hell. A hell that was burned, shredded, smouldering, baron, desolate and now absolutely lifeless.

She sighs as she reflects on seeing the large chunks of broken land and the dry dusty air scorching her throat. It's like a boomerang, she fumed. You chop it down, fling it away and it comes back and whacks you on the back of your head. That's deforestation and climate change in a nutshell. Everybody will get an environmental boomerang whack on the back of their heads. Katty purses her lips and thinks about what they could do in their next campaign. Thank goodness for Miss Violet and her samples – evidence of pollution for all to see.

* * * * * *

Miss Violet gently crouches down to the ground. She pincers a pair of tweezers to carefully lift up a handful of pollution samples. Some of the samples are charred tree and some are small clumps of soil. Miss Violet places the samples into separate sample containers. She holds each filled-up container to the beaming rays of light and squints to inspect them while twirling the containers in between her thumb and index finger. This, Miss Violet nods, is evidence and proof. These samples are precious specimens and useful to carry out some classroom science experiments.

The smoke and the soot is ever present. Miss Violet captures the smoke in a jar so she can do a science experiment and present her test findings back at Brumfield Primary School. She would also use the sticky window cards like she did for capturing carbon dioxide (CO_2) from the car exhaust fumes outside the school. The smoke is filled with black, stinking toxic soot. The smoke splutters, coughs, taints, stains, smears and chokes the air we breathe. In the end... everything is polluted.

Miss Violet peers deep into the microscope's lens as she softly twirls the focus wheel with her thumb and index finger. The microscope lens zooms in on the glass sample slide and the view expands into a larger focus. Miss Violet's eyes expand and widen. She can see the pollutants wriggling, squirming and swimming in a drop of solution on top of the sample slide – some pollutants were doing breaststroke, other pollutants floating on their backs with their arms and legs spread out like a star. She could see the guilt in their teary eyes. At least she hoped it was guilt in their downfall. Miss seethes through gritted teeth at the destruction these pollutants had inflicted on the rainforest.

* * * * * *

'I'm not a celebrity, get me out of here,' yells Deeco. 'Let. Me. Go.'

Miss Violet can't hear him, but she can just about make out his beetroot screaming face. Under the microscope lens, there was Deeco's outlined sooty body with arms and legs poking out. Germie has to suffer his raging shrilling tantrum. He is always whinging. His throat burns, he wheezes and pants. Germie's head rings, pounds and throbs. It was no use, he frets. He was stuck and trapped in the gooey solution. His bleary bloodshot eyes bulge. The teardrops spill out and roll down his cheeks. His shoulders rock, he balls out into sobs. He can't move and will have to wait to be disposed of again. Germie rolls her eyes. Pathetic, she vexes.

'Oh, rubbish!' shrills Deeco. 'It's happening all over again.' He always ends up being stuck on a microscope sample slide. He can't see her, but Germie is floating nearby, stony silent. She is embarrassed to be exposed to the giant eyeballs looking down on her. She is ashamed to be seen with Deeco.

Deeco has been in this position before, same location, same eyeballs. Here he is again, lying down stuck in gooey liquid, unable to move. He lay deathly still. And here he is again, pancake-flattened on top of a slab of microscopic glass. He glares with his crazy eyes up into a massive microscope lens that is beaming down at him with a pair of mega humungous eyeballs gawping down at him. He recognised the eyeballs. He recognises Miss Violet. His whole skin prickles in rage and he clenches his jaw.

'Really? This is happening again to me. It's really humiliating,' babbles Deeco. He was stuck and had nowhere to hide. The eyeballs moved up, down and *across as they gawped at him. He was being judged. Who was she to be judging him? It wasn't illegal to be a pollutant. At least he didn't think so. But he was being held captive against his will.*

'I have my rights,' he shouts in protest as loud as he could bellow it out.

'We don't have rights, you stupid fool,' growls Germie. 'We are pollutants who pollute. We violate our rights because we contaminate the air, land and sea.'

Well, perhaps she had a point, reflects Deeco. Perhaps he didn't have his rights. After all, he was in no fit state to say he was clean. He was anything but clean. He was a dirty pollutant, that he couldn't deny!

Miss looks to Katty and beckons her to have a peek down the microscope's lens. With a keen grin Katty virtually leapt across like a young gazelle.

'Oh, awesome, Miss. I think I recognise some of these pollutants from the car exhaust fumes from outside Brumfield Primary School.'

'These pollutants certainly do get around, Katty,' quips Miss. 'That's for sure.'

'I'd forgotten how tiny the pollutants are. There are loads of them,' said Katty as her eyes stare into microscopic binocular lenses. 'They are tiny, but poisonous like invisible, toxic ninjas.'

They fester. They pollute. They destroy.

The thoughts spin around Katty's head – *fester, pollute, destroy*. These black ninja dots on the microscopic glass slides are more proof of the pollution all around us, everywhere and on everything.

CHAPTER 13

COP Bravo

Jake padded along the wooden floor in his beige woollen socks and flip flop sandals, grinning at the prospect of being at an important meeting with both Miss Violet and Sergio. The last meeting had just been him and Katty at home in the kitchen.

This meeting would be in the dining area in the communal eco-cabin. A table food buffet was already set out. The sweet scent of fruit wafts across the room.

Miss Violet sat at one end of the long table with Sergio and Jake with a solitary lonesome Katty sat upright and perched opposite them. But she was close enough to Miss so that made it all right as far as she was concerned. This would be Miss Violet's and Sergio's first Climate Summit meeting. It would be the second Climate Summit meeting for Katty and Jake.

Jake rummages in his rucksack for the typed up notes from their first Climate Summit in a kitchen in the world famous town of Redditch. He and Katty shuffle their bums on the wooden bench on either side of the dining table and rustle and unfold their stapled notes. It was official and they were ready. Katty had typed up all the written notes they had done. She had had time to read up on their notes and she knew what still had to be done and who was to do what. She hopes this climate meeting was the time for further progress. Progress matters, now more than ever. She saw the news on TV and there was always bad stuff about the climate. She puffs out her cheeks. *Phew!* Her chest fills with pride as she pushes her shoulders back. She sits to attention and clasps her hands together, interlocking her fingers in prayer... and in hope.

Sergio had settled down onto the bench next to Jake. The long, chunky rectangular wooden table in the canteen cabin is an ideal meeting place. Sergio rubs his hands in excited anticipation of attending his first formal Climate Summit meeting. He felt important. He will be representing Brazil. Sergio was standing in for the present Brazilian President, Lula da Silva.

Miss Violet's eyes beam through a determined gritted grin. The adrenaline of excitement surges through her body. Her body shudders into a jolted burst of exhilaration. She reflexes with an impulsive clenched right hand into a shaking fist.

'Yes,' she hollers, 't-t-t-ti-titaaniiiuuum.' Her cheeks redden a light shade of pink. She immediately realises she hollered a little louder than she had intended. A stunned silence falls around the dining table. Jake, Sergio and Katty gawp at Miss wide-eyed and open-mouthed. There is a few seconds pause, and then they all burst out laughing. Miss joins in laughing too.

Miss Violet chairs the meeting and Jake decided he was happy to sit next to Sergio for *brotherly* support. Miss was mentioning the good work Sergio was doing for the rainforest and that she hopes her sample collection will benefit their school in Brumfield, Redditch and be the springboard to launching their rainforest campaign.

'That would be very good, Miss Violet,' said Sergio. 'It is always good when tourists and scientists come to visit. They see the *real* problems and the *real* deforestation for themselves.'

'Sergio, you can call me Zoe.'

Jake's eyes pop out of his head. He darts a glancing look at Sergio and smiles and then he immediately turns to Miss Violet with a wry grin.

'Oh, um,' murmurs Jake, 'can I call you Zoe too?'

'No, Jake,' lightly barks Miss, 'you cannot.' She gives Jake a pretend scowling narrow-eyed stare. 'You can call me, Miss.' And with a nod of her head Jake gave a slanted, dimpled, apologetic grin.

'Comprendo… understand?' prompts Miss.

'Yes, Miss,' mutters Jake. 'I comprendo.' He bows his head to stare at the ground. Sergio chuckles to himself. Katty smiles inwardly. She always enjoys it when Jake has a telling off.

'Me comprendo too, Miss,' pipes up Katty, pleased that Jake had had his comeuppance at last. *Serves him right, the cheeky little worm.*

'Yes. I comprendo too, Miss,' cackles Sergio. They all giggle and smile, much to Jake's relief.

Mum and Dad were excluded from the Climate Summit meeting on the grounds that the *'oldies'* did not understand climate change stuff, so they were allowed to go on a *date night* thing. Embarrassing oldies behaving so badly, looking into each other's eyes, and kissing. *Urgh! In public too! They had no shame!* Katty and Jake flash a startled look at each other and pull contorted, gut-wrenching faces. Mum and Dad cuddling and kissing is disgusting and yukky. *Show some respect to your children!* Huff Katty and Jake.

Today's schedule was all about the Climate Summit meeting. This meeting is their very own version of the Conference of Parties (COP) as held by world leaders every year. This is COP-time. Katty and Jake did their COP-time Climate Summit meeting after every expedition. It meant a new campaign too.

'Everything is inside out, upside down. Nothing is in the right order,' Katty whispers to herself. The cogwheels in her mind turn, clunk, clink and whirr around as her brainwaves try to make sense of it all. The same conclusion hits her time and time again. It just seems so obvious, doesn't it? People should look after the animals and trees and plants and water; the ecosystem should then look after the land and sea. But no, she chided. It was too much to ask that people and businesses do *not* need to pollute the air, the land or the sea. And why not? She flings her arms up in the air. Because it affects everything... including the people themselves. *How stupid are people?* She puffs out her cheeks and sighs.

Miss Violet had mentioned a big meeting in the UK called the Conference of Parties, written as 'COP'. It was called COP26. It is the twenty-sixth COP meeting where all the big world country presidents and prime ministers had met and promised to fix the Earth's overheating climate. *Fix? Really?* Even Miss raised her eyebrows thinking about all the world leaders and politicians making empty promises and telling big fat lies. It was glitz and glamour of fake enthusiasm and environmental pledges. Just like the previous twenty five COP meetings that had been held in different cities all around the world. Miss Violet sighs heavily. They have held the twenty-sixth COP meeting in Scotland. It is held every year, and it is still not fixed, but getting worse! Miss recalls the president of COP26. He was shedding tears. She wondered if they were fake tears or the tears of a clown. Or was it fake clown!? A lie is a lie, even if everyone believes it. She wondered was it so obvious that a clown must make the public believe him. He weeps the politicians' betrayal and they do not have an ounce of guilt. It would be different at *their* Climate Summit meetings. Words mean campaigns and campaigns mean actual actions, Katty decided.

Katty and Jake would add their own conference to their own Climate Summit agenda. Who needs big meetings in Rio, Paris, Glasgow and Sharm el-Sheikh? Katty and Jake had used their *glitzy* kitchen at home for their first Conference of Parties (COP) meeting which meant action with their school 'Stop Idling' campaign to tackle excessive car exhaust emissions. That was COP Alpha. This time they would in an Amazon rainforest eco-friendly log cabin for their COP Bravo Climate Summit meeting and then there would be another meaningful campaign.

Miss Violet lightly claps her hands to get everyone's attention.

'I formally open this Climate Summit meeting and announce the start of our very own version of a Conference of Parties,' declares Miss with a wry smile. 'The difference is, we do not need the political world leaders to attend. This is the second Conference of Parties event and is to be known as COP Bravo.'

Jake's arm shot up into the air.

'This is after the first Climate Summit meeting with me and Katty, Miss. That was called COP Alpha,' utters Jake excitedly. He nods to Sergio who smiles back at him.

'Yes, Jake, and of course we had our very successful 'Stop Idling' campaign on reducing car exhaust emissions outside of our schools,' said Miss.

'And, um, err,' huffs Katty, her eyebrows knit down in a frown, 'the campaign will have *real* action by *real* people who actually care about the environment too.'

So, another thing to come out of today's Climate Summit meeting will be what campaigns they will be doing once they get back to Brumfield Primary School in the United Kingdom. Katty knew their brains would be working hard. Katty also knows it will make Jake's stomach rumble, so Miss had arranged a buffet for after the meeting. Katty could smell the sweet crunchy, crispy, coconut shortbread biscuits, the delicious banana-filled pancakes and luscious chocolate juice.

Lovely-jubbly, as Mum would say, imagines Katty.

Sergio had whispered to Katty and Jake, as they were about to sit down, that a surprise spokesperson from the jungle would be calling in to discuss issues on behalf of the animals. *Who could that be?* wonders Katty. She knew of no spokesperson. Nobody had mentioned a spokesperson for the animals before. With her elbows propped on the table, she cupped her chin into the palm of her hands.

'Where had this spokesperson been all this time?' murmurs Katty to herself. *Why would the animals need a spokesperson and why had she not been told about this before?* Something wasn't right. She had her suspicions that Sergio and Jake were up to something. A practical joke maybe, she frowned.

Miss Violet chairs their overseas Climate Summit and as a special guest, Sergio is invited to attend. He is honoured... Jake beams at Sergio. He thought that he and Sergio could be in a TV advert for the campaign, cosying up a cool bromance scene, tackling the loggers and illegal farmers and ranchers from chopping and burning down the rainforest. *Yeah, how cool would that be!?*

Jake boasts to Sergio that the FOTD – *Facts of the Day* – is his idea, and he got the idea from the football television highlights programme *Match of the Day* (MOTD).

'Yes, that's a very clever play on words Jake,' chirps Sergio eagerly. Katty didn't think Sergio was convincing in calling Jake clever, but Jake just laps it up like a little puppy dog wagging its tail.

A silent mystical, eerie draft sweeps the across the room above Katty's head. Something in the air swoons majestically above their heads in a silent, swishy, wafting whoosh. Whatever it was it seemed to possess an authoritative and determined presence. Did that mean spooky or chilling? ponders Katty.

Who would be seen as possessing wisdom? What authority would be needed to blame those who destroy the rainforest? Katty had often thought about who should be in charge of the impacts on the environment, but she had never managed to quite grasp a clear image in her mind. It was so obvious, she conceded. Why hadn't it been thought of before? It didn't have to be the Mystrees 'walking, talking trees' of the Amazon rainforest or Gandalf the Wizard of *The Lord of The Rings*. No, no. The image was sat right there on the far end of the table right in front of her. There was no mistaking it. It had wisdom and authority. The owl had been nominated to represent the whole of the planet's animals so that *their* voices could be heard too. The owl had a clear vision of unbiased judgement on behalf of the Amazon rainforest and especially representing the animals.

The owl hen was sat on the empty end of the Climate Summit's meeting table. The opposite end to Miss Violet. Katty peers unblinkingly at the owl. She, the hen, is an owl. Not just any old owl. No, no. She is a *wise* owl. A legal court *judge* to be precise. She was wearing silver-brimmed spectacles perched on the top of her short pale white downward-facing curved beak. She wore a long black robe and a white, lacey ruffle neck collar on the front of her blouse. A bright white, flat bib drapes to her front; the bib looks a bit like a large bow tie.

The presence of the owl was spookier than chilling. *How odd?* Katty frowns.

Perched on top of its head is a white tight-curled courtroom wig that dangles down either side of her head like long flappy ears. Katty rubs her eyes. What she saw was an owl dressed as a courtroom judge.

Not only could she see it; she could hear it too! A talking owl!

'Wowzer, Sergio. You don't have to be Doctor Doolittle to be able to talk to *all* the animals,' exclaims Katty. 'The owl is talking to us!' Katty couldn't help but stare at the owl dressed in its legal outfit. Katty blinks. The owl is wearing a black robe, a ceremonial white curled wig and spectacles perched on the end of her beak. The smartly dressed *talking* owl introduces herself as Judge Amber Green.

Judge Green blinks a squint and gives a curt nod. Katty thought an owl blinking meant 'go away'. *That's rude!* Katty's head buzzes. She can actually see and hear a *talking* owl. Was she going mad!? Was it real? Could anyone else see and hear the large white and grey owl? The Judge puffs out her fluffy feathered chest as she sits majestically at the head of the table. Sergio, Jake and Miss Violet are all transfixed, their jaws hanging in shock. *Okay*, hoots Katty. This was definitely real.

Judge Amber Green sits upright and heaves out her fluffy chest again as she shuffles her position on the end of the table. She shudders her feathered body and tootles her words as she makes her legal case against the loggers, farmers, miners and governments. She gives her verdict and passes her sentence on those for punishment. Katty has no doubt – they were all definitely guilty.

Katty's lungs inflate with renewed hope. Nobody will be ruffling this owl's feathers, Katty muses. She has respect for this amazing owl. She hadn't seen that coming! Judge Amber Green will definitely offer wise words on behalf of all the animals suffering because of deforestation. That will certainly get the attention of anyone in the Climate Summit meeting.

Judge Amber Green clenches her feathered hand to keep a tight grip of the dark brown, wooden 'hammer' gavel. The gavel 'hammer' came crashing down onto the table in a thunderous clitter-clatter of repeated bangs on the tabletop. Miss Violet, Katty, Jake and Sergio gasp. Their breaths dissolve into silence. All their eyes stare to the commanding owl sat at the end of the table with an awe of authority. Nobody dares speak.

'Order! Order!' hoots Judge Green. Her head swivels from one side to the other. The Judge's head rotates. She eerily scans the whole room. Her big black velvety pupils in her large, round, yellow eyes peer intently over the silver-brimmed glasses perched on her pale yellow beak. She pauses a glance at each and every person around the table. Katty can't help but look directly back into the owl's spellbinding, mesmerising eyes. Katty gulps. She felt a rush of goosebumps prickling her spine. She wants to shake her head in disbelief as she sits upright and gawps, open-mouthed at this astonishing spirit, this ghost, this vision. Her brain just can't compute that there was an owl dressed in legal robes and a white wig. And it was talking! It was just like *wow! Gobsmacked!*

The owl rocks gently from one foot to the other.

'Thank you, members of the Climate Summit meeting, for your services to the environment. Okay, Miss Violet, Sergio and the little environmental kiddies, let us consider a few important facts,' twirps Judge Green. *That's a bit rude*, frowns Katty, she wasn't a *kid*, but she supposed she would let it slide this time. It was obviously meant for Jake!

Judge Green bows to read from the paper scroll of notes she had laid down on the table in front of her.

Ahem. She clears her throat with a short cough.

'Members of the Climate Summit,' she lightly barks. 'Based on the facts and evidence in this case, I have come to a decision.' She pauses, rolls her shoulders, puffs out her feathers and juts out her beak. 'I pass judgement on the world leaders, politicians and corporate businesses for their neglect and failure to protect the Amazon rainforest.' Judge Green's eyes narrow to a flickering squint. She sucks in a lungful of air and exhales slowly. 'I summarise that these world leaders, politicians and corporate businesses are only interested in the *greed* in their profits, egos and self-wealth. They are only interested in the *feed* in supplying excesses of beef and not for the people living in poverty. They are only interested in the *bleed* in destroying the rainforest in deforestation and pollution.' The irritation in the owl is simmering. Puffs of steam whistle from her pointy ears.

'Greed, feed and bleed,' she honks a throaty, gravelly growl, grinding her beak. Judge Amber Green's tone was a definite gruff scowl – filled with anger and scorn.

Katty fumes inside at the thought of the continual cycle of *greed*, *feed* and *bleed* being allowed to go on and on, around and around, again and again and again. Her brain whirrs, her head twirls around and around just like the disheartening desperate thoughts that are turning the cogwheels in Judge Amber Green's mind and churning around and around, clunking, clinking and whirring, again and again and again.

'Please remember,' snuffles Judge Green, 'whatever the defendants have said is *not* evidence. The evidence is trees being chopped and burned down. It is vandalism and pollution. These all lead to climate change, storms, floods, droughts and fires.'

'I can conclude that the defendants...' She raises a pointed feathered finger. 'And just to be clear, the defendants are the world leaders, governments, big business polluters and, of course, the polluting loggers, farmers, ranchers and miners,' she hoots gruffly. She huffs an exhale of breath and puffs out her speckly tan, brown and white feathers. Katty notices that Judge Green looks bigger and more menacing now.

'These criminals have been proven to be guilty beyond reasonable doubt. In fact, without any doubt. In fact, let there be no doubt at all. Guilty. Guilty. Guilty.'

Katty senses the air around the room crackling as the tension rises.

'Members of the Climate Summit, you have heard all the testimony concerning this case. I have judged the evidence. I have determined the facts. I have decided the evidence and facts prove the criminal acts of deforestation and so prove the neglect of the planet, Earth.' Judge Green puffs out her feathered chest. 'I have therefore reached a verdict. I say the world leaders, governments and politicians are guilty of allowing this destruction and pollution. I thank myself for reaching the guilty charges and I thank you, the Climate Summit members, for your attention today in receiving my judgement.'

It is a welcome judgement, but it wouldn't make any difference for now, considers Katty. But still, the animals would be very happy their judge owl has said so.

Miss Violet, Sergio, Katty and Jake clap their hands like a group of puppy seals, smiling and nodding their heads towards Judge Green. She nods back, twitching her pointy ears. A silence follows and the judge sinks back down into a seated position and the Climate Summit meeting restarts. The meeting continues with FOTD. The table is scattered with scribbly notes and the facts are blurted out with excited squeals by Katty and Jake.

'Did you know?' chips in Sergio. 'Twenty per cent of oxygen in the world is produced by the Amazon rainforest.' He is a bit unsure whether he should be officially stating any facts. But he was entitled, of course, thinks Katty.

'Well, then. That's a good reason to stop the wheezing lungs of the Earth,' blurts Katty. 'Seriously, definitely worth doing.' She quickly utters that the rainforest actually spreads across nine countries. *Nine! How mad is that?*

'Really?' grunts Jake. 'It don't sound right to me.'

'It is right. It is defo nine countries,' retorts Katty.

'Next *Fact of the Day*, please,' huffs and laughs Jake, but he didn't feel the need to bite back. 'The Amazon river is the longest in the world. It is a whopping

4000 kilometres long,' he huffs a chuckle. 'That's a lot of swimming the lengths of the swimming pool!'

'Crikey!' gasps Sergio. 'Really? I didn't know that.'

'Yes, really,' quips Jake, 'It's a true fact 'cos I said so!'

Sergio winks to Jake that he agreed.

'Deforestation accounts for thirty per cent of all global carbon emissions,' grumbles Miss Violet. 'And that's not all. The forest could be gone in forty years.'

Sergio's face dropped in shock and horror.

'The height of the Iguazu waterfalls can be between 60 metres and 82 metres. It is a fact,' Jake nods cockily. 'The Iguazu Falls is nearly three times as wide and twice as high as Niagara Falls.'

'We already knew that. Stupid!' hisses Katty.

'Yeah, but it's still a fact. So there, even stupider!'

Jake rattles out some more facts. The Amazon is the river; Amazonia is the forest or as Jake called it, a jungle; Amazonas is the region in Brazil which owns sixty per cent of the forest land. Jake chuckles. He was so chuffed at his compilation of *Facts of the Day*. Sergio applauds, grins and nods his approval. Jake beams.

Jake declares that he thinks there will Artificial Intelligence (AI) carbon catching clouds hovering above in the sky, like big mega-ginormous atom-magnetising vacuum bags sucking up all the dirty pollutants.

'Really? You really think that's a fact,' pricked Katty. 'A real thing, is it?' Her eyes narrow.

Jake wasn't sure if it was confusion or was his sister just irritated? He presses his lips tightly to consider his response.

'No. But it could be,' he insists with a nod of his head.

Katty raises her eyebrows.

'Huh!' she huffs. 'Pigs might fly!'

A flutter of wafting feathers rustle as Judge Green fans her wings. 'I would like to add a *Fact of the Day* before I depart,' hoots Judge Amber Green. 'Cattle ranching makes up eighty per cent of deforestation in the Amazon rainforest.' Miss Violet, Sergio and Jake turn to each other, nodding their heads approvingly. *Oh, okay*, pouts Katty. She was actually going to use that *Fact of the Day* for herself. Not to worry. It sounded more convincing coming from an owl judge.

'Yes, your honour,' squeaks Katty with a nod. She hadn't meant to speak; her thoughts just came out as words. Her mind boggles in a fuzz. She frowns. This was so weird, so strange, so bizarre. She was agreeing with the opinions of a *talking* owl!

Katty thinks Judge Amber Green has a lot of authority and a straightforward opinion on everything. The Judge reminds Katty of somebody else. Katty shudders and cringes. That somebody else was Jake but Jake had *no* authority, and yet annoyingly he definitely had an opinion on everything.

Judge Amber Green grips hold of her wooden gavel and taps down onto the table to an echoing *clack-clack, click-clack*. It was her way to address an end to her part in the Climate Summit meeting. She rolls up her scroll and tucks it neatly into an inside pocket of her robe. Before Katty could blink her *thanks* to the owl, the judge had drifted up from the table in a hovering flutter and swooned out of sight through the cabin's window.

Whooooosh! In a flickering swish and swoosh, the owl was gone.

Katty blinks, raises her eyebrows and pressed a tight-lipped grin to herself. She hastily scribbles down squiggly notes from what the owl judge had said as best as she could remember. She would type up the notes back at home and in school and print them off to be kept safe and file them tidily in her green clip folder. The folder consists of neatly typed up notes by Katty. Mum had insisted on checking for any spelling mistakes. Katty carefully inserts the notes into recyclable poly-pockets labelled on the front of the folder in thick black permanent marker 'CLIMATE SUMMIT FOLDER'. Multicoloured dividers separate each Climate Summit meeting, and each was marked for each exploration and campaign event. So far, there had been their first Conference of Parties, spelled as COP and they had named it COP Alpha. This had been for the carbon dioxide car exhaust emissions campaign and now they were doing COP Bravo for the deforestation of rainforests and all trees in general. They would raise awareness of deforestation and use Miss Violet's Ambassadorial influence on a campaign to plant loads of young tree saplings at schools all over the world, if they could reach that far.

CHAPTER 14

Scorchio!

The Climate Summit meeting was going well. The owl judge had been an awesome surprise and Miss Violet, Sergio, Jake and Katty had sat upright and paid close attention. They continued the meeting and decided that a 'choking lungs of the Earth' awareness campaign would be the way to go. Miss nods her words to Katty, Jake and Sergio.

'The overheating, burning planet Earth is *scorchio!*' said Miss. 'Be chilled, live on a less hot planet'. Katty thinks this could be a campaign slogan.

That would only be part of it, Miss declares with glee in her eyes and rubs her hands eagerly. She announces that there will be a tree planting campaign too.

Katty's mind wanders back to the depths of the Amazon rainforest's trees. She feels she has made a connection with the ginormous spider-legged Kapok trees, especially the walking, talking, grumpy Spike and chilled-out Lofty. She'd felt their pain and anxiety at the deforestation of the trees. She'd feel even better to be part of such a heartfelt tree planting campaign that Ambassador Violet was determined to roll out to all the schools in the UK. That was the power she had as the Climate Sciences Ambassador for Schools. If she couldn't get it done then nobody could, supposes Katty. *You don't mess with Miss Violet.*

The message would be that planting trees is a great way to help suck in the carbon dioxide from the air. The awareness drive is that through photosynthesis, trees absorb carbon dioxide to produce oxygen and grow the wood.

'It's a "win-win" to grow the trees and suck up the carbon dioxide,' chirps up Katty with a nod to Miss Violet. Miss grins her approval.

Miss Violet's campaign drive is to plant trees in all school locations and anywhere she is allowed to by local authorities, if she can get away with it. The little baby trees to be planted were one year old saplings called high quality 'whips'. Miss explains that the campaign helps greatly to provide wildlife with new habitats, and support biodiversity, and offsets the naughty carbon dioxide (CO_2) emissions that happen all around us and all around the world. She pulls a sad face with a downturned mouth, then gives a nod and a smile with a determined fist-shaking gesture to get stuck into their tree planting event.

'Remember,' calls Miss Violet with her clenched fist, 'plant a tree and so help protect the planet.'

Miss Violet's buoyant enthusiastic energy fills the eco-cabin's room. She would take that same energy to the lush green fields while crooning the lyrics *'we are titaaniiiuuuum'*.

Titanium rocks!

'Planting trees is part of our campaign. The Amazon rainforest is the lungs of the Earth. We must campaign to stop the wheezing lungs, the choking forest,' teems Miss Violet through gritted teeth. She will strive to plant trees in their local schools, hillsides, parks, gardens and even generate new forests.

'There are plenty of places to plant more trees,' said Katty, nodding her head towards Jake in particular.

'Where?' puzzles Jake. He rolls his eyes and shrugs his shoulders.

'Everywhere!' hisses Katty. She could feel her face burn with rage. The little worm was winding her up good and proper now, she fumes.

'Maybe we could even plant trees in the pavement,' quips Jake.

'I'd like to plant you in the pavement,' Katty growls.

Jake raises an eyebrow. *Gotcha!* he smirks.

Ahem, coughs Miss. Jake and Katty look at her apologetically. They look with sad eyes to Miss, but with no regrets or apologies to each other. *'Cos that's what siblings do.*

This campaign will actually involve planting trees. No surprise there, thinks Katty. Planting trees on a ginormous scale, like between 90 and 120 million trees per year... all the way up to the year 2030.

Wowzer! Now that was a surprise.

It would definitely be knackering, thought Katty. *Eeeek!* Bend back, dig a little hole with a shovel, pop the tree in and pat it down again with the shovel. All those trees. *Creek!* Knackering, achy back, blistered hands. But it would definitely be worth it too. Imagine all that super-duper photosynthesis carbon dioxide yomping going on and the trees pumping oxygen back into the air. Fresh, exhilarating and breathable. That would help stop any chance of the country's lungs choking, let alone the Amazon's lungs of the Earth.

The Mystrees, Lofty and Spike, are always nearby, skulking around and guarding the rainforest. Katty, Jake and the other tourists annoy Lofty a little and everything and anything fills Spike with irritation and scorn. They didn't call him 'spiky' Spike for nothing, muses Lofty. Lofty had softened his opinion of the little girl since he had witnessed Katty showing concern and anger at the plight of the rainforest's survival. Katty cares. Katty wants to help. Guilt prickles Lofty's crinkly bark skin.

'Perhaps she isn't so stupidsy after all,' concedes Lofty with a lopsided grin. Spike peers across to Lofty and considers his remarks with suspicion.

'They still don't belong here though,' snaps Spike.

* * * * * *

'Okay, everyone. That is the close of the Climate Summit COP Bravo,' says Miss with a warm comforting smile. Katty looks directly across to Sergio and Miss with pleading eyes. They both nod. Miss gave a sympathetic dimpled grin. That was as good as a promise that they will do what they can, Katty supposes in hope. A promise to try and make a difference. Nobody, it looks like, can promise to stop the mindless, selfish, heartless destruction of the rainforest. It will have to do for now as Katty presses her tight-lipped grin to Miss. She felt the tears spill on her insides, so nobody else could tell that her real fears for a future without a rainforest pinged and prodded at her heart. The pain hurt really bad.

She feels as though the Amazon rainforest's lungs of the Earth were suffocated and that she is the one to revive their breathing function. *Breathe Lofty, breathe Spike, breathe rainforest*, pleads Katty's mind. She sucks in a deep breath, filling her own lungs. She scowls a determined, squinted narrow-eyed stare at the paper with the written words and notes of their meeting as it lies flat neatly across the table.

I need to give this my best shot, she urges herself. She needs to do her bit too, so does Jake, so does everybody. This girl was going to join the army of determined, honest, hardworking campaigners on a mission to stop the planet burning up. She was going to do it without her own hair plaits, like Greta Thunberg's plaits, but she would most certainly do it with the same attitude and willpower. The world needs to know what is happening. Yes, why not... be mean, be green. Jake frowns and looks across at Katty. Her eyes were all squinty and starey like she was glaring into space. She'd gone into one, daydreaming, away with the fairies. *Typical girl*, he jests. She was probably thinking about shopping or thinking she was beating him at Mario Kart. He claps his hands.

'Hello, Katty!' Jake clicks his fingers to wake her up. 'Are you there?' he sniggers.

Katty snaps out of her dreamy trance. Her shoulders jolt. She startles jumpily.

'Huh!' she quakes. 'What? Yes, of course I'm here. Is that the end Miss? I'll write up the notes later, if you like.'

Miss and Sergio smile and nod their approval.

'Yes. That would be lovely. Thank you Katty,' replies Miss in a soft, soothing tone.

If Miss Violet can do things to better the environment as a science teacher and Sergio can guide people to see the good over the bad of the rainforest, then Katty wonders what she can do to help when she is older. She guesses Jake will play Super Mario with *Mario* and *Luigi* darting around in their hydrogen-powered and environmentally friendly aeroplane karts. The aeroplane karts putting out rainforest fires and *Yoshi* and *Toad* driving solar-powered tree planting tractors in deforested areas in the rainforest. Katty smiles at her wild thoughts. She knew that hydrogen power releases zero carbon dioxide emissions. Katty leans her head to one side and purses her lips in serious thought.

'Mmmm,' Katty hums out loud. Maybe she could be a solar power design engineer or make artificial intelligence clouds that magnetise dirty, stinking pollutants from the atmosphere.

* * * * * *

Katty sits on the steps to the cabin. Sergio was relaxing and gently swaying in his hammock on the veranda of the cabin next door. Jake had attempted to copy Sergio and climbed into their own hammock. As he unsteadily and wobbly plonks himself onto the hammock, everything and everyone spun full circle and he rewinds back halfway and then Jake drops down onto the wooden-planked veranda floor with a heavy thud.

Urgh! A bruised Jake sits up rubbing the back of his head and his right elbow. Katty ignores Jake's bumbling and groans. She watches the sunset as the sun sinks below the horizon between the distant lanky trees. The shimmering red, yellowy-orange streaks frizzling out on the horizon.

'That's weird,' she thinks out loud in a croaky whisper. It reminded her of the embers of another forest fire.

The sun would slowly be doused out by the gravitational pull of the moon, yawning its illuminous torchlight presence into a darkening slumber. The flickering midges buzz and speckle beneath the forest canopy and the creepy crawlies scuttle into the nocturnal cycle of life. Goosebumps prickle her skin, shivering down her spine. She gulps at the thought of all those creepy crawlies slithering over her in the middle of the night. *Urgh... Yuk.*

'Brrrr,' she shivers, wrapping her arms around herself. The air was light and breezy. It would be time for dinner soon. The menu choice for tonight was stroganoff. Rice served with meat in sauce. *Mmmm, lush!* Or another choice is Jake's favourite – a selection of different pizzas and potato chips.

Katty and Jake huddle in a secret chit-chat. They criss-cross letters and words with sketches and scribbles. Pencil scribble – rub it out; pencil scribble – rub it out. Katty and Jake scratch their heads, frown, bite their lower lips. They can think of loads of good stuff but were finding it difficult to put it into words and sentences. Homework wasn't as difficult as this, they both stressed. They keep thinking of good things to write. They had decided to write a leaving speech letter as a 'thank you' to Sergio.

Jake holds the folded sheet of paper in front of him. His sweaty palms shake, the paper creasing between his clasping fingers. He looks up. The small audience to him is a blur. He inhales deeply, lifting his chest and exhales a murmur through his nose. Sergio, Mum and Dad come back into focus. He lifts his chin and, without looking at the sheet of paper, he booms out both his and

Katty's experiences and memories in the jungle. Katty winces. *It's not a jungle Jake, you prat!* She silently urges him to read the speech like they had agreed. She tries to catch his attention, but he is looking straight ahead. Mum should telepathically tell him. But Mum didn't and Jake rambles on loudly with a bumbling 'thank you' to Sergio.

Katty ponders about the things the owl, Judge Amber Green, had said about greed, feed and bleed. The corporate businesses' *greed* is to sell too much, so the people buy too much, and then waste too much. All to make profit, Judge Green had sighed.

Katty fidgets her fingers and wrings her hands in despair.

The *feed* is people to eat more and more meat and so throw away more and more food waste. All this comes with concerns because she knew and witnessed the loggers, ranchers and farmers *bleeding* the rainforest by cutting and burning down more and more trees to farm the land. She huffs. And yet still, there are more and more starving people and food poverty in the world. She groans a sigh. She just can't figure it out. The greedy big corporate businesses have figured it out though and they make vast profits because the governments allow them to.

Sergio scrunches his eyes in a deep frown. *Mmmm,* his mind whirrs. But nobody is paying any attention to the rainforest being chopped down, burned and the land flattened to grow crops and feed cattle to produce beef burgers.

Sergio had spat out *greed, feed* and *bleed.* He had explained that there were no other reasons to this never-ending destructive deforestation other than sheer *greed* for profit, *feed* for piggishness and *bleed* to *contaminate* and strip away the land and pollute the air that we all breathe. Tears roll freely down from Katty's stinging eyes. She wants to sob, but what would be the point in doing that. It felt useless and hopeless. Her blood boils and even then she must take a deep breath to fight off the sizzling anger. Fireworks were going off inside her head. She can't let it get to her like this. She needs to calm down, she was being too loud. If only she was like Taylor Swift. So cool; so calm. Katty takes a deep breath and sighs heavily. Her shoulders slump. It was all getting too loud. A clear head was required so she could think straight. It never works with Jake because he was a pain in the neck. Mummy's boy. Katty gazes into the distance, searching her mind for answers. What would Miss Violet do? Miss always had a solution and was always calm.

'Only two sleeps before we go back home, so make the most of each day,' exclaimed Mum as they sat down for breakfast. Jake potters around the cabin, his rucksack packed and ready to leave the jungle. His heart aches and feels heavy in his chest. Each heartbeat squeezes his chest tightly. Each breath drains the air in his lungs. His legs wobble like jelly. He must sit down on the edge of the bed. His whole body trembles and quivers. He steadies himself, planting his hands down onto the bed. *Okay*, he urges, *breathe, Jake, breathe*.

The hard drive in his brain hums and whirrs as his breathing steadies and his heart relaxes. He furrows his brow to a deep frown as he tries to collect his thoughts. The cogwheels in his brain clunk and clink as one thought surfaces and it triggers another thought. He daydreams. First, there was the image of Brumfield School and it made him cringe. Then another train of thoughts clicks into place, one after another. His head whirrs a little lighter and the hum was not so soft and quiet. He was in a cool, cosy house and the air was not sticky and humid and it was mosquito-free. *Chillax*, he urges. *Clunk, click.* The cogwheels continue to effortlessly intertwine into an image of a hamburger in a bap, and he could see himself, a chilled-out Jake, lounging on his bed and playing Mario Kart with no interfering Miss Bossy Big Boots (Katty), and hopefully no head-shaking Mum either to tell him to do his homework or clean his bedroom. His whole body oozes in a dreamy delight.

Awesome!

After he had chomped on his hamburger and whizzed around a few laps of Mario Kart, Jake sighs a heavy groan as the daydream melts away and he finds himself back in reality, back in the rainforest. He blinks and purses his lips. He was going to miss Sergio. He was like a big brother to him. He wondered if he could swap Katty for Sergio. It was a 'win-win' thing, he grins. He would be happier with a new cool older brother and Katty would no longer get on his nerves, and be bossy, and snitch on him to Mum and Dad, and grovel to Miss Violet. The other day, and in front of Sergio, Katty had even called him 'titch', no taller than a skirting board, she had chuckled. Jake's face reddened as he fumed. Sergio didn't get it, but *he* did, and he wouldn't forget it either.

'Just wait until I am taller than you, big sis,' he murmurs. Then she would be 'titch' and he would be 'lofty'!

Katty arcs the torch beam ahead of her from her chair on the cabin porch. The torch light sweeps ahead like a prison's searching strobing spotlight. The torch beams brightly, illuminating the darkness around the campsite. Katty gasps and startles when the light catches shimmering eyes in the trees close by. The menacing eyes are staring straight back at her. She can't make out if they belong to a human or an animal. Why are they looking at her? Were they carrying out surveillance for an attack? If it was an abduction, she ponders, can't they just take Jake and leave her alone? *Oh!* she trembles. What if the Yeti had come back? *Oh, flippity-flip!* She freezes. She was almost breathless in shear panic. Her lower lip quivers, her chin juts up and down.

'Help us, please, Mystrees,' croaks Katty as her thoughts came burbling out of her shuddering mouth. Her rapid blinking eyes sting and she gulps. 'Lofty. Spike. Please help,' she pleads. 'Don't let the Yeti munch us up.'

The minutes pass by and Katty slowly realises her mind had got carried away. She'd had a moment of hysteria, she concedes. If there were any peering eyes, it was innocent enough and nothing was going to munch her up. Jake might be munched, but not her! She catches her breath away from any peering eyes in the forest and decides to step inside the cabin and sit on her bed.

Her galloping heartbeat cantered down to a trot and eased to a more relaxing walk. *Clip clop, clip clop.* She twiddles her thumbs and reflects gloomily at the heavy burden of her experience in the rainforest. Her heart sinks deep into the yawning pit of her tumbling stomach. Down, down and down, further still. It felt like an endless tumbling fall of hopelessness. Her head buzzes at the enormity of the challenges ahead and she wonders if it wasn't already too much to change. Judge Amber Green had wanted change too. A stop to the need for greedy profits, the need for endless piggish feeding and the reckless result to bleed the Earth of its trees and land and to pollute the air.

Katty gulps and closes her eyes.

Images swipe across her inner eyelids like a cinematic slideshow. Her lips squeeze a tight-lipped strained grin. She recalls seeing Miss Violet pointing to the transparent carded windows as part of her experiment to catch the sooty pollutants that was used to promote the need for the 'Stop Idling' campaign they did for the school car traffic, spewing out disgusting exhaust fumes. Not for the first time, she knew. She didn't care who it was who were responsible for the smouldering jungle and choking enormous lungs of the Amazon rainforest. All she did know was that it had to stop. It had to stop if we wanted to breathe. It wasn't too much to ask, she huffs in disbelief.

Every time she saw the worldwide news and weather headlines every day it was obvious to her to see that because of climate change there is the excessive heat, the raging fires, floods and droughts happening everywhere. She sighs a heavy sigh as she was not sure that the world leaders and politicians would take any real notice. The politicians spurt out a plan to give great hope and expectations. Typical fake heroes dressed in sheep's clothing. Katty fumes. It made her blood boil so much that steam might spurt out of her ears.

The heroes should be the world leaders, politicians and big businesses. They are the ones who should drive forward environmental changes but instead they do the opposite. They deliberately dither, stifle, pollute and break promises. Yes, chides Katty, *they lie and lie but the mirror never lies. They are the problem. Everybody agrees. They should be the heroes, but no, they are the villains.* Katty wondered if only she could root for an anti-hero. Taylor Swift sang about an anti-hero, recalled Katty. Maybe she would know what to do.

COP-time, Katty tuts in dismay. She puffs out her cheeks. Every year a Conference of Parties (COP) event is held between world leaders, and nobody really agrees, and nobody really does anything. It is exhausting. Katty definitely feels exhausted, waiting for the world leaders to do climate change stuff... and do it now. *Who can possibly save the planet?* Katty doesn't know who the anti-heroes are she should be rooting for? Could the anti-heroes be the consumers? Could these people who buy excessive and luxury items change their habits to be anti-heroes and start buying more sustainable foods and clothes and ways of travel? Having a 'green' conscience was not always enough, concedes Katty. The consumers could change their habits, and this would encourage the villainous polluters to stop polluting and clean up the mess.

'The heroes always let you down,' grimaces Katty through gritted teeth. Those world leaders and politicians that should be influencing climate change to save the planet are allowing big corporate businesses to ravage the rainforest for profit.

Written words; spoken words. World leaders and politicians promise everything; words are cheap.

Empty words more like, Katty seethes. The days, weeks, months, and even years pass by with very little action. Written words on a piece of paper are all they produce. Sign the paper and then they just think 'that's that'. It is just a piece of paper that is signed by political world leaders and somehow celebrated as a great achievement. The same old climate change declarations and promises are idly shifted from one COP Summit meeting to another, passing the baton on as the baton gets hotter and hotter. *Blah, blah, blah*. The *déjà vu syndrome*, as Miss Violet called it. It wasn't an illusion. It was the same excuses for not stopping the pollution happening over and over again and again and again. Katty blinks heavily. Grits of distress speckle her eyes.

Everybody suffers in the end; it's just that everybody doesn't have a choice to change it. The choices are with the governments, and they choose not to see it as a problem. They choose to ignore it and pretend to be doing something. All they do is kick the 'tin can' further down the road. *Not everybody chooses to ignore it*, huffs Katty. Somebody needs to stop kicking this 'tin can' down the road. Katty and everybody else knew that the further the 'tin can' gets kicked down the road, the worse it gets. She sighs. At least she knew that with each of their own Climate Summit meetings and with each campaign, it takes on more and more importance with less and less time to stop the pollutants taking over the world.

CHAPTER 15

The Long Goodbyes

The last dinner passes by with teary eyes, silent awkward pauses, and giggling laughs as they recall the ups and downs of their adventure. The expedition gang of four: Sergio, Katty, Jake and Miss Violet munch and chew on the main dish of the evening – grilled tiger catfish enwrapped on a luscious green leaf. The environmental motley crew stay hunkered around the food bench, swapping stories and ideas.

Mum and Dad were on another date night and were glad not to be babysitting.

'Really? Don't they understand their parental duties?' huffs Katty.

With no Mum and Dad around to discipline them, Katty and Jake guffawed and sniggered as they told tales of Dad's brave, but not so brave, blood donor fainting episodes. And, of course, Mum's chocolate obsession with brownies, her secret hiding places and how Dad always had a telling off if any went missing. They promise to keep Sergio up to date with their campaign to save the Amazon rainforest and planting trees.

Jake drinks the large jug of orange juice in one long guzzling slurp. He exhales his delight and his shoulders sag in satisfaction.

'Buuurp!' belches Jake. He swipes the back of his hand across his mouth and gives a blushing grin. *What a disgusting pig*, scowls Katty in a frosty silence. He was lucky Mum wasn't nearby, or else he would have had a telling off and told to say 'sorry' too.

Katty stares intently into a blank space as the cogwheels in her head clunk, splutter and whirr a jumble of thoughts around her brain. Her stare turns into a gloomy gawp. The penny dropped in her mind's eye and it struck her in surprise. *Oh wow!* she thought. She had just realised that over the last week in the jungle, and under the guidance of Sergio, that the term *guide*, as he was known, was so unfair. Sergio was far more than just a guide. He had a talent for tracking a path through the thick dense jungle in all weather conditions. He can whisper to animals and trees; she was sure of that. Katty knew he had a passion for the survival of the rainforest. He had proven that with his teary eyes of anger, pain and despair. She knew he was environmentally conscious of what the destruction of the rainforest meant for him, for Brazil and for the rest of the world. And, of course, he was a buddy to Jake. She cringes. And that took some doing being a buddy to Jake. That meant that Sergio had to be patient, tolerant and put up with Jake's cheating. Katty presses her lips to a dimpled grin. Most of all she saw Sergio as a friend, someone she too could trust. She thought that Miss would vouch for Sergio's many talents too.

* * * * * *

Katty absolutely loves seeing the rainforest in all its splendour. She even sort of liked its eerie spooky mystique. Her mind beams like a bright fluorescent bulb, but the joy was always tinged in a shimmering ray of sadness. The projector in her mind switches on and shone brightly. The lens bulb illuminates the images inside her head. Some of the images she would rather not see but couldn't help; it reminded her of the destruction that was really happening. Images she would keep and store for a long time to come. Beauty, sadness and hope.

The same old story of greed, feed and bleed rang out in her mind. Katty realises the sadness was that she had to leave the deforestation behind her when she left. It makes her feel empty. She felt like they were deserting Sergio too.

She exhales heavily. One minute she is breathing in the soothing scented aroma of trees and leaves and flowers; the next minute, there's a disgusting stench. Katty wrinkles her nose and gets the whiff of a pungent gagging odour. Was it the smell of rotten eggs? Had Jake farted again? Or was it manure?

Yuk! she gags and coughs.

She wonders what it means. Sergio gives her a lopsided grin. *Well, that doesn't look good*, she thought. That's because it isn't good. Not good for the nose. Sergio recognises the disgusting eye-watering stench. It belongs to the hoatzin, a pheasant-sized bird with an enlarged crop (gut) in its throat and it was hiding somewhere nearby. Its honky-squawky hiss echoes around the campsite.

'It digests its food in its throat which is why it has really bad breath. And that,' explains Sergio with a grimacing grin, 'is why its nickname is "stinkbird".'

'Oh gross!' Katty and Jake cringe in unison. The smell is a proper yuk-yuk, gut-wrenching stink. Sergio grins.

'High fives!' shrieks Jake.

'Toca aqui!' chuckles Sergio, slapping his palm against Jake's palm.

Katty rolls her eyes. She recalls and recoils at the tangy, burning charcoal smell mixed with the sweet aroma of sizzling tree sap as it hits the back of her throat, choking and gagging. She didn't think the smells and images would ever fade away in her mind. Her nostrils had twitched and she had sniffled, more in reflex than actual sniffing. The imagines of the dying wood embers still seem to tinge her nostrils.

The evening brought in a warm, musky but fresh aroma, tinged with butterscotch and vanilla. It filled the air. It's the smell of life. If she could bottle it up and spray it as a perfume, it would be awesome.

Katty doesn't want her last night dinner and chit-chat to ever end, but she knew it would have to. Her heart clanks, clangs and chimes inside her ribcage. The more she thinks about leaving the jungle, the more her heart pings and bounces around. The wrench of leaving Sergio to tackle the deforestation on his own didn't feel right. It was a funny sort of aching pain that she doesn't like but knew she had to accept and get used to it. Sergio will be fine, but Katty realises it will be worse for Jake.

Katty's eyes dart quickly to above her head. A swooning flutter of flapping wings swish through the air in around the nearby trees. She can't see any birds flying so she wonders if it is the owl, Judge Green, checking in on her. She squints and scans in and around the tree branches looking for a white wig, a long black gown, a silky white lacey ruffle neck collar and a hammer gavel.

Nothing! tuts Katty. She was sure the owl was there somewhere.

Judge Green, the owl, stays as still as a statue as she is perched on a branch. She peers over the top of her spectacles, down at Katty who is looking up into the trees. She hadn't been spotted.

Katty smirks a dimpled grin. The owl had had a presence of authority at their Climate Summit meeting. It had been a shock to Katty when the owl started talking but now she knew that Judge Amber Green was the real deal. Katty was impressed. *Awesome!* she enthuses. A wise, honest owl. The owl spoke on behalf of the animals of the rainforest, and she gave them a voice to say that the animals mattered too. The animals needed saving from the deforestation – the destruction of their habitats.

The time to leave the Amazon rainforest and this exciting adventure was getting closer. It made Katty feel hollow inside, her heart deflated. She sat lost in her own thoughts for a moment. She imagined Dad patting her gently on the top of her head. It was his way of saying 'it's okay, don't worry.'

* * * * * *

The dark sky, speckled in tiny white dots, turns grey and slips into the night. Then the sky turns yellowy as the night slips away and the sun burns through the sunrise. It is time to say their goodbyes to Sergio. Sergio hugs Katty, Mum, Dad as if it was the end of a beautiful friendship. It wasn't. But the thought of not seeing him tomorrow and every other day twangs Katty's heart strings. Sergio gives Jake a heart-warming, sad, joyful, teary hug. Jake clings on... and on and on. Eventually, Sergio pats Jake lightly on his back. Jake's head emerges from Sergio's chest. The cute little boy Sergio kidded as 'fofo'. Jake doesn't look so cheerful, cheeky and bright. Jake was red-eyed, and he felt broken and fragile inside. A forever big brother, Katty felt. She knew Jake would swap her for Sergio in an instant if Mum would allow it. Katty hoped Mum would not allow it.

Katty takes one last look at the Amazon rainforest through her stinging tear-filled eyes. She glazes at the beauty it portrays and at Sergio's encouraging strained smile. Were those tears she could see in Sergio's eyes too? Her mind's eye flickers a clattering of snapshot stills on a film reel, and she blinks through them, spilling a tear at each clip – the charred tree stumps; grey ashen grounds; skeletal bones of perished animals, and weeping bubbling sap spilling from the tree stumps. Those tree stumps could one day be Spike and Lofty, she scolds.

CHAPTER 16

New Little Mystrees

Katty's mind hums the putrid smells and sweet sickly scent of the sap. *Urgh!* She was having flashbacks. The traumatic images of deforestation play on a repeat cycle every so often in her head. She gulps and blows out a heavy breath. The images weigh heavy on her heart. She sucks in a lungful of air through her nostrils, gulps her throat and exhales a release of her anguish. She would have to get used to these shocking scenes of environmental sabotage, she frets, *'cos this is what it is like in the beautiful Amazon rainforest.*

The humidity in the air had gone and it had been replaced by a cool chill. It was a 'hello' as a return to Brumfield Primary School beckoned. A strange sadness was also replaced with a deeper sense of determination and a new campaign, headed by Miss Violet. Katty smirks, she was honoured. Take a bow, Miss Violet. Take a bow, Ambassador Violet. The one and only Climate Sciences Ambassador for Schools.

Miss Violet had attended a big meeting in the school with counsellors from Redditch Borough Council for approval of their new campaign to plant trees in chosen fields and woodland areas.

Katty and Jake sit still in the empty school corridor as the footsteps of Miss echo on the vinyl floor. She is walking towards them. Katty notices a glint of joy in Miss Violet's sparkling eyes. It was definitely good news. It meant the campaign could go ahead. Katty manages to suppress her vocal cords from squealing. Her whole body inside shrills with excitement. *Oh my gosh!* She might even have wet herself! she jokes to herself. Her head whirls at the thought of planting five million trees. FIVE MILLION! It was actually going to happen. Plant five million trees. Her feet began to shuffle up and down like a penguin doing a *Happy Feet* dance. Miss Violet smiles.

'T-t-t-titaaniiiuuum,' her gargling tonsils ring out. Katty and Jake rock up alongside Miss and join in chorus.

'*You shoot me down, but I won't fall; I am titaaniiiuuum-um-um-um-um-um.*'

Miss, Katty and Jake nod their heads in unison to each 'um'.

'*I am titaaniiiuuum-um-um-um-um-um.*' The quivering tune echoes down the corridor, bouncing off the shiny, pale blue vinyl floor and light grey glossy walls. It was a proper vibe and Katty thought that the permission from the local authority to plant trees in loads of areas was something to be pleased about... but it was only the start. She knew that Miss Ambassador Violet had ginormous ambitions to plant and plant and plant more trees. Miss would make sure that so many other schools would be spreading their campaign far and wide, school by school, county by county until all of the United Kingdom was done. Katty enthuses at the idea of hundreds, thousands, and hundreds of thousands of trees that will be planted to help the lungs of the world expand in support of the Amazon rainforest.

Planting trees would be like growing little saplings like Spike and Lofty, but not the size of the Kapok trees.

'Maybe we should go back to the Amazon rainforest and plant trees there too,' she mutters under her breath. Katty didn't really fancy the idea of walking, talking trees wandering around Brumfield Primary School! She smirks as she remembers the eerie spooky whisperings in the misty jungle and even then, Spike and Lofty would be complaining about something and bickering between themselves.

* * * * * *

In the distance on the adjoining field earmarked for a mass of trees to be planted, Katty could see *Jake the prat* bobbing up and down. He was quite elevated and springing quite high up into the air, much to Katty's confusion. *Huh!* she frowns. He wasn't normally so athletic and sporty; he was normally a lazy worm. Then Katty realises that he was holding onto a very springy, bouncy pogo stick. Why was he prancing up and down on a pogo stick? *Oh*, she suddenly realises, maybe he was a teeny-weeny bit brighter than he looked. Katty notices that attached to the bottom of the pogo stick was a spiky hollow tube and so each time he bounced up and back down, he was actually prodding a hole in the soil. The hole in the soil meant someone could come along and plant a baby one year old 'whip' tree sapling into the ground. Katty thinks, *clever prat!* as she bites her lower lip.

* * * * * *

Miss Violet's rucksack has a circular blue and green global 'holiday' sticker on it with a red print inscription 'Wish You Were Here' splurged across it. The irony was not lost on Miss Violet as the rainforest wasn't exactly pollutant free, she grimaces through gritted teeth and a scowl. Katty can sense the titanium of emotions bubbling up inside her – nobody was taking her down. It was going to be an awesome campaign back at school. The Climate Sciences Ambassador for Schools for the whole of the United Kingdom would be leading the campaign.

Katty's chest flutters and her brain floats in delight. She was so chuffed about the super-duper Miss 'Ambassador' Violet. Katty knew how Mum felt now. Mum always felt thrilled when she turned off the oven to reveal her super-duper brick-sized knock-out whopper chocolate brownies as they sizzle and tiptoe dance on the baking tray.

Miss taps the microphone with her index finger and utters words into it. The microphone squeals with jarring screeching feedback.

Eeeeeee-ee-ee-e.

The screeches pierce her ears. Pride can be a peculiar thing, Katty declares, scratching the side of her head, and frowning. Miss taps the microphone again.

'Testing. Testing. One, two, three. Testing.'

Katty clasps her hands tightly together. The whites of her knuckles burn. She bounces on her tiptoes. *Flippin' heck!* she thought. Did she want a pee? She could feel her insides crumbling under the volcanic pressure swirling around her tummy. Her heart pounds, thrashing against her ribcage. Now she feels lightheaded, dizzy and a bit wobbly on her feet. She sways a little.

Oh, flippity-flip!

Katty just might faint. She huffs. Dad was the fainter, not her. He couldn't give blood without making a big dramatic fuss. The blood service nurses must have felt sorry for him. They even gave him a red heart-shaped badge after he fainted so many times!

Katty could hear Miss Violet continuing to tip-tap the microphone, *testing, testing,* and counting out loud; *one, two, three, four.*

'Testing. Hello,' calls Miss to no-one in particular as she taps and speaks into the stage microphone. 'Calling planet Earth. You are getting hot, hot, hot. The Earth is burning, burning. The smouldering temperatures and fires can be seen from outer space.' Miss Violet hisses ironically. She was getting quite poetic and rhythmic, thought Katty. Katty even thought for a moment that Miss would break into song.

'Testing, testing, one, two, three.' And then all the poetic testing had been complete.

Miss nods with a confident grin towards Katty. Katty slowly shuffles along the solid, polished wooden flooring. The soles of her rubber-soled trainers lightly squeak as she makes her way from behind the tall, draping purple curtains at the back of the stage. She steps into the spotlighted area in front of the assembly hall. The assembly hall seemed bigger and louder from high up on the stage. The spotlight would be on her. Expectant eyes would divert from Miss Violet to Katty Sheehan. The butterflies whoosh up from her stomach into her throat. She gulps hard to clear the airway.

A surge of adrenaline lifts her chest. She had to speak up; she had to provide the evidence. Katty's emerald, green eyes flicker in a moment of panic. She steps from behind Miss, adjusts the microphone down a little closer to her mouth. She takes a deep breath. She grips the sides of the lectern, her hands clenched, her knuckles whitened as she grasps a little tighter as if to hold herself up. She was standing behind the wooden lectern in front a swarm of students in the school assembly hall. She stands proud in the centre of the stage but her body trembles with prickling fear and burning excitement.

She gives a hard steely stare and juts her chin out.

'First, I'd like to say thanks to our guide in the Amazon rainforest, Sergio, for his expertise and passion to preserve the rainforest. Next, thanks to Miss Violet and to Jake, my little brother for all his help. Also, I would like to thank you all today for attending this launch of the school campaign in our mission to help save the Amazon rainforest.' Katty remembers to blink away her steely scary stare as her fellow students look up to her above them on the stage.

It was *her* who was giving a presentation. It was *her* that was on stage. Okay, it wasn't exactly in front of world leaders, politicians and corporate bigwigs, but she was on stage in the assembly hall of Brumfield Primary School and all the pupils were present and peering up at her. She was explaining climate change to her school at morning assembly. This was proper mad.

Miss Violet looks on with pride.

Rock it, girl.

Miss Violet's mind buzzes with pride, and she can hear Sia singing in her mind. Warbling vocal cords ring out loud, echoing out in her ears. She hums the lyrics as they gently echo in a whispered tone.

'You shoot me down, but I won't fall... I am titaaniiiuuuum,' she whispers. Miss could see Katty was growing from a Brumfield Primary School student into a confident young person. She will be a future ambassador to look after the environment. Katty is strong and resilient; she *is* titanium.

Katty's passion spills out from within her, she can feel a course of adrenaline rushing through her body. It gives her that urge – an unexpected, renewed confidence somehow, and a purpose. It's a slow burner but it's increasingly taking a hold on her. She was even beginning to think of choices she could do in the future like studying science, meteorology or teaching like Miss Violet. Anything, she proposes, that would help the environment and where she could still campaign for a better world. The buzz of interest from the assembly hall is inspiring. Katty realises there would be no shortage of volunteers, especially if they could make it feel more like an adventure and that everyone would be making a difference to the environment and saving the lungs of the Earth.

* * * * * *

The pollutants drift up and up. Noxic swirls around in sideways loops and finds himself drifting upwards. Upwards! he frowns. The air is less black, and he is slowly drifting higher and higher. He is not alone. He is one of thousands and thousands of other dirty, stinking pollutants, aimlessly drifting up and up. The air is less smoky. He can see the smoky black twirling clouds below him. He can see and hear the burning, crackling, sap spitting trees below being consumed by the raging fire.

Polloo puffs out her cheeks and wipes the soot from her blackened panda eyes. She squints and flutters her eyelids. She can just about make out Noxic floating in the mass flock of other pollutants just above her. Clickety-clunk! Clickety-clunk! her brain murmurs. She didn't understand what was happening. Why were they not landing on the trees and the ground? They should be polluting the rainforest, but they weren't. She smiles in relief. She felt glad.

Noxic's body lifts higher into the air. The trees in rainforest below are looking smaller and smaller. He was a long way up! His eyes catch the sight of Polloo. His eyes plead to her for some comfort. He hopes it will be okay, he believes in hope. He was glad he was not going to pollute the rainforest but is so confused. His slanted grin twitches, his quivering eyebrows lift up onto his forehead. Polloo can sense his unease. Speckles of sweat trickle down his forehead. He wipes his warm, tingly forehead and puffs out his cheeks. He starts to pant and wheeze. He didn't know what was happening and nor did Polloo. Where were they going? Where did going upwards end up? They were being sucked up high into the atmosphere. They could end up deep into outer space and get sucked into a black hole.

Aargh! Gulp! Cripes! He was getting proper stressed now.

'Polloo,' croaks Noxic, 'I think we are being sucked up into a black hole.'

He can see the strain in the eyes of Polloo staring back at him. Polloo sighs as her body drifts higher and higher. Her eyes glisten, her heart sinks. There are hundreds of thousands of other pollutants swarming around them and they were all heading up to collide and punch holes in the ozone layer.

'The ozone layer acts as a sunscreen and protects the planet from the hot sun rays,' Polloo vexes gruffly. 'The holes in the ozone layer let in loads more hot sunrays.'

'That means the planet is too hot, right?'

'Exactamente!' nods Polloo. Noxic frowns.

'Exacta-what?'

'Exactamente means exactly,' sneers Polloo. 'The planet is too hot.' Noxic bites his lower lip and scrunches up his face in a grimace. He thinks in deep frowned thought for a moment.

'So, it is like living in an oven,' he mutters.

Noxic grasps Polloo's hand. They both realised they were still pollutants and they had been released into the atmosphere to pollute the ozone layer. Noxic squeezes Polloo's hand.

'We don't deserve to be pollutants,' he murmurs. 'Polloo. It's not our fault.' He shakes his head and looks up to the distant ozone layer above. He feels guilty at what he was about to be a part of. Nothing could stop it now. The ozone layer was getting closer and closer. Noxic and Polloo hold on tight to each other and tightly close their eyes.

Oh, what a disaster! frets Noxic.

Bang! Bash! Thud! Crash! Thwack!

✳ ✳ ✳ ✳ ✳ ✳

Katty and Jake knew they could make a difference. They had done it before. They had to stop the parents in their cars spewing out pollutants from their exhaust pipes while idling their engines before and after school. Now they were looking at planting trees to help suck out stinking carbon dioxide from the air and telling the real story of the awful destruction of the trees in the Amazon rainforest. Katty presses her lips together tightly.

'Let's get mean; let's get green,' she murmurs. She pouts her lips. She was determined it wasn't going to stop here either. With every expedition she did, she would doggedly make public their discoveries and campaign to rid the planet of the stinking, wretched pollution. She could feel she was making a difference. She had to make a difference or else what was the point.

Katty veers through the school's echoey corridors and steps outside into the school yard. The hustle and bustle of the school hall fades into the background. The rush of adrenaline fizzles out of her veins. The normal chaos and mayhem of break times in the school yard was devoid of screeching students and yelling, yodelling teachers.

Make sure you keep your feet on the ground, young lady, so Miss Violet had said. Miss Violet's words chime and ring in Katty's ears. Katty was determined to keep her feet on the ground. She smirks a dimpled grin because she knew where she was going on her next adventure would mean that her feet would definitely not be planted on the ground. She'd be floating in the air!

Woohoo! she gasps. Her whole body whoops inside.

She couldn't keep her feet on the ground in outer space. *Outer space, outer space,* her head echoes. Her whole body tingles, and a shudder ripples up her spine. She blinks, sucks in a lungful of air, gulps and exhales to release her excitement. Her eyelids droop shut for a few seconds as she collects her thoughts. She gave a relaxed, sighing grin. She opens her eyes with a crooked smirk. She leans her head back to look upward and squints a prolonged gaze way high up into the skies and beyond.

'Yes,' murmurs Katty, 'I am looking at *you*, sky.' She is peering up – way, way up high beyond the clouds and she feels like her inner spirit is soaring high up into the atmosphere and even higher up into outer space. She firmly plants her feet down, slightly apart and places her hands on her hips. Her chin juts out with a sense of determination. *Oh my gosh!* This could be a *Buzz Lightyear* pose, she realises. Her laser-like stare zooms in towards the stars with a steely-eyed squinted glare.

'Next stop is the stratosphere. Our next adventure is to travel up to the ozone layer,' instructs Katty as she nods towards the stars. 'I've heard there is a problem that needs addressing. I'll see you soon.' This was going to be an expedition into space. *Mmmm*, she ponders. *This would need a space shuttle to fly into space.* The space shuttle would have to do twirly circles, flippity-flips and loopily-loops to orbit the Earth. This might be one way for them to tackle the many punctured holes in the ozone layer.

Katty lightly taps her index finger onto her pursed lips. She frowns in deep thought. Maybe they would need someone to fly the space shuttle too. And any mention of space Jake would say, 'to infinity and beyond'. Jake is a bad loser, and a prat, as Katty would say. She stands upright and looks up to the skies.

'To the ozone layer and beyond,' roars Katty as she punches her clenched fist into the air. 'Watch out,

Buzz Lightyear! Watch out, pollutants.' Katty plants her hands on her hips, purses her lips and juts out her chin. 'Enviro Kids – space suits on,' she barks, 'rocket boosters on... we are on our way.'

Milton Keynes UK
Ingram Content Group UK Ltd.
UKHW010008260624
444713UK00001B/17